I0764619

Vision in the Forest

Michael Goldman

illustrations by Miss Lauren Altman

Order this book online at www.trafford.com
or email orders@trafford.com

Most Trafford titles are also available at major online book retailers.

Printed in the United States of America.

ISBN: 978-1-4269-3337-0 (soft)
ISBN: 978-1-4269-3338-7 (hard)
ISBN: 978-1-4269-3339-4 (ebook)

Library of Congress Control Number: 2010908387

Our mission is to efficiently provide the world's finest, most comprehensive book publishing service, enabling every author to experience success. To find out how to publish your book, your way, and have it available worldwide, visit us online at www.trafford.com

Trafford rev. 7/28/2010

www.trafford.com

North America & international
toll-free: 1 888 232 4444 (USA & Canada)
phone: 250 383 6864 • fax: 812 355 4082

Table of Contents

Note: Historical references for this novel were gathered from *The Sagas of Icelanders and Wilderness Messiah* by Thomas R. Henry

To my loving Wife Charlotte,

To my Grandmother Violet Bergendahl
for all her teachings of the forest,

To my Stepfather Merle
Goldman for all of his support.

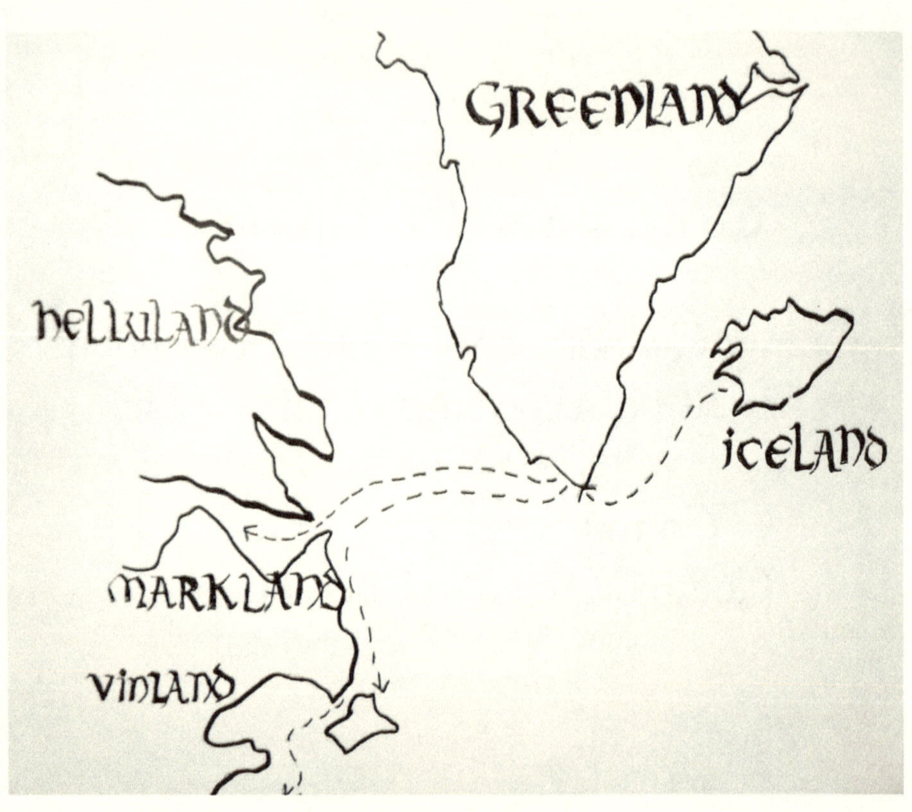

Voyages to Vinland

Prologue

Around the year 1000 A. D. Norse adventures made several sea voyages to the North American continent. They were a hardy breed of men fearless in battle, born with a lust for life and the unknown. Their ships bore the proud dragonheads carved on the bows of their ships, sailing to most of the known world, trading, conquering, and settling many lands; these were the Vikings.

Our story concerns one special young man, a Viking through and through, born with that lust for adventure, even stronger than most. It is the author's desire to impart some small history of these early Viking voyages to North America before introducing to you the central character and his vision for peace among all men, especially the native men of the forest.

It all began with a man named Bjarni trying to reach Greenland from Iceland. He was blown off his course due to vicious north Atlantic weather. As his ship neared some land after a strong storm, he and his crew noticed green forests and hills--land that they had never seen before--and it certainly was not Greenland with its ice-capped mountains. As the winds were blowing them away from shore, they never attempted to land being eager to reach their destination in Greenland. They finally reached their port and upon telling people of what they had seen they received quite a lot of criticism for not landing and exploring this new land.

One man listened well to the tale and determined to find this new land himself. His name was Leif Ericison, a large strong man of very striking appearance and wise as well, being a man of moderation in all things.

He purchased Bjarnis' ship from him and gathered a good crew of like men for the voyage. He named his ship Skidbladnir after the gentle god of Norse mythology, the god of the sun and the rain. He asked his father, Erik the Red, to make the journey with him. Erik was getting on in years but was willing to go. On the way to board the ship he fell from his horse and was badly injured. He decided not to make the trip and spent the rest of his days at peace on his farm in Greenland.

Leif boarded his ship with thirty-five good men for his crew, one of these was a man named Tykir from a country south of Norway. They put to sea, making the crossing from Greenland. The first land they spotted was flat with glaciers, a land like a big slab of rock, useless to anyone. Leif named it Helluland, meaning stoneland.

They put out to sea once again and came upon a second land. They cast anchor, put out a small boat and rowed ashore. This land was flat and forested, sloping gently seaward with many white-sand beaches. Leif named this land Markland, meaning forestland. After exploring a little Leif and his crew returned to their ship and put to sea again. For two days they were at sea with a northeast wind. Coming upon an island they went ashore again where they found fresh early-morning dew on the rich grass. They cupped their hands and drank it having never tasted any thing so sweet before.

After this they sailed into a sound where the ship became stranded as the tides went out. They would not wait for the tides to turn desiring to reach the land ahead of them. When the tide floated them free they towed the ship with their small boat and then rowed the ship up a river where eventually they cast anchor in a lake. At first they carried their sleeping bags ashore but as they desired to stay for some time exploring this land they set to work building two stone, long houses on the beach. Leif put his men to work gathering stones that were plentiful along the waters edge. These they placed tightly together forming two walls with a space for soil in between to help insulate the building from the cold. Then using stout poles for a framework, they laid large chunks of sod for a good solid roof. A smoke hole above the fire pit allowed smoke to escape from the heating and cooking fires. All in all the houses were warm and comfortable.

There was no lack of salmon either in the river or the lake, salmon larger than they had ever seen before. The land seemed good, the temperature never dropped below freezing. This meant fodder all year around for their livestock. The days were much more equal than in Greenland or Iceland; in the dead of winter the sun was aloft by mid morning and was still visible at mid afternoon.

Leif divided his men into two groups, one to explore and one to stay by the houses. No one was to travel so far that they could not return the same day. This they did for some time. Leif went on these explorations sometimes and also stayed by the houses to keep a watch on their ship for they knew not what kind or manner of men might be in these lands.

One day the southerner, Tykir, was missing. Leif was very upset over this. Tykir was one of his father's oldest friends and helped take care of Leif when he was a boy. He picked twelve men to accompany him in a search. They had gone but a short way from the houses when Tykir came out of the woods very excited. They greeted him warmly. He was a short, frail man but skilled in all types of crafts. "Why were you so late in returning, foster father, and why did you get separated from your companions?" Leif asked.

Tykir was so excited rambling on in German which no one could understand, his eyes darting all about. He finally calmed down some and speaking in Norse said, "Grapes and grapevines, the forest is full of them, of wild grapes like where I grew up."

The next morning Leif told his crew they would cut timber one day and gather grapes and vines the next. Soon the small boat they towed behind their ship was full of grapes.

When spring came they headed out to sea with a full load of timber and grapes. With favorable winds they came in sight of Greenland and the mountains under its glaciers. Leif named the land where they found the grapes Vinland, meaning wineland. Leif hoped to encourage other Greenlanders to make the journey to his newfound land to settle and build their farms. Such a good productive land would mean plenty for all and an easier life. As they neared home Leif spotted a ship in trouble, sinking close to shore. He sailed straight for it to help the men on board if he could. There were fifteen men about to go into the freezing waters, which would have meant certain death. Leif took them all on board his ship saving their lives. After this he was known as Leif the Lucky. Leif found places for all these men to winter until they could find a ship to return to Iceland in the spring, the land they called home.

Not long after this Leif's sister approached him about making a trip back to Vinland. This then is where our story begins--the tale of one young Viking, only eighteen years of age, but a man with a vision ahead of his time.

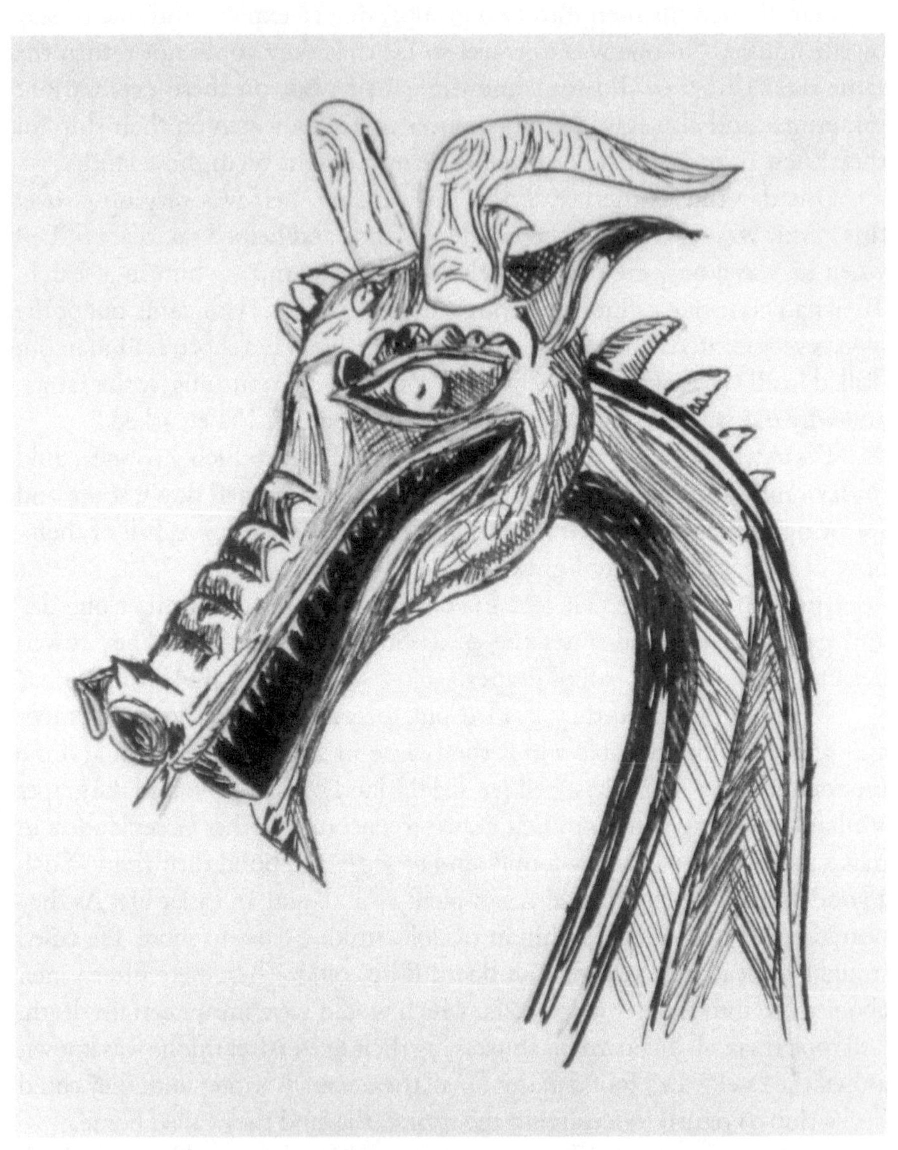

The Feared Dragon Head of a Viking Ship

Chapter 1

Around the year 1002 A. D. a stout Viking longship, its huge sail billowed to its fullest, crashed through the rough North Atlantic Sea. The well known and feared dragon head on the prow seemed to challenge the winds to do their worst, for neither ship nor the men on board would be deterred by mother nature.

This ship was on its way to the new world lands discovered by Leif the Lucky a few years before. Two brothers, Finnbogi and Helgi, owned this vessel. They meant to cut timber which they would sell for a handsome profit upon returning to Greenland. It was late winter, the winds and seas were very cold. As the salt spray spewed over the men toiling with the ropes and sail, their beards and hair coated with ice. This was second nature to a Viking for they were born to the cold and took it in their stride.

At the helm steering the ship, was a young lad of eighteen years, tall and muscular, his yellow hair blowing in the wind and his blue eyes flashing with excitement. He was Thorfinn Oakenshield; this was his first adventure away from home. He worked with his father on their farm in Greenland but upon hearing of this voyage about to be made by the brothers, he fervently sought permission from Leif to go along. He thought now on how he had rushed to Leif's farm to ask permission to go on the journey. His father bid him well for he knew the adventures nature of his son. He would not be able to keep him farming forever. As he topped the last little hill above Leif's farm he ran down to the house and banged on the stout oak door. Leif was home from working his fields and he opened the door not surprised to see Thorfinn standing there. He had already heard of the young lad's desire from Thorfinn's father the day before. "Leif I must talk with you," he began, "I wish to make the journey with Finnbogi and Helgi to the new lands. I'm sure they will have me if you give your approval. Grant me this favor and I will forever be in your debt." He looked straight at Leif as he spoke hoping to impart how much it meant to him. Leif put his hand on Thorfinn's shoulder and answered him straight away. "You are a strong and able man for one of your years. I know you to be an agreeable man without a bad temper. If this is what you wish, I will speak to Finnbogi in the morning for I believe you will be a strong asset to them. It is a dangerous journey with many unknown things still to be discovered. Men like you are needed to explore and settle it. I hope to see many of our people living there someday; there is much more to that land than just timber to cut for a profit. You shall go, I promise. Come inside and let us raise a horn to the journey." The two men entered Leif's home where his wife was waiting with two full horns of strong Viking ale, which she handed to the both of them with a big smile. "If I didn't have to stay here to look after all the people now that my father is unable to do it anymore, I would go again myself. Perhaps you will be my eyes and tell me of all your adventures when you return." After speaking these words Leif raised his horn and drank it dry before putting it down. Thorfinn thought he must be the luckiest man alive at this moment.

He was already skilled with his weapons and the stories told by Leif and his men aroused in him a desire to see the far-off forestlands, a desire so strong he could fight it no longer. Now here he was about to sight the new land at last, an adventure few men in this time could imagine. Thorfinn felt strong; his strength surpassed that of many seasoned Vikings on this ship. Only he had been able to hold the helm straight in the rough seas they had just crossed.

On his back he carried his grandfather's sword, Grasida--the gray blade said to have an ancient Celtic spell on it. As long as the bearer of the sword wore the scabbard, he, too, would be invincible in battle. Thorfinn believed in this legend; it had been passed down from father to son for generations in his family. Thorfinn was a happy man; he had just become a Christian, turning away from his old god, Odin. Leif the Lucky had been asked by King Olaf of Norway to convert all the people of Greenland to Christianity, the new religion spreading across the lands. This suited Thorfinn well as he was a man in love with life and nature. He would defend himself and others if necessary, but a world of peace instead of war and killing was his desire. It would take time for the old myths and gods to die, but he would try.

As the winds and seas subsided, a shout of land to the leeward rang out. All hands rushed forward straining to have their first look at the giant green spruce forest. Men shouted, giving thanks for a safe crossing, staring in disbelief at what lay before them. Quickly the men lowered the sail. Manning the oars they rowed the ship towards the beach. They were in a calm, glass-like sea now, the ship's reflection adding to the beauty around them. Their course on the voyage over had been true, for the two stone houses built by Leif still stood strong on the gravely beach in front of them. Securing the ship by stout ropes tied to trees they unloaded the ship's supplies needed on shore: water, food, clothes, and tools. Then they began the task of making the houses secure from the elements once again. Thorfinn looked in wonder at these stone structures still standing strong as the day Leif had built them. He wished he could have been here to help those who built them. Several of the crew discovered a freshly-beached whale a short ways up the shore, a lucky find indeed. Now they would have fresh whale meat to last them for some time to come. Finnbogi had the men move their tools and food supplies inside the houses. There were thirty men altogether, fifteen men to a house. They settled in to wait for another ship that had departed Greenland with them; that ship was bearing the sister of Leif the Lucky. Her name was Freydis and her husband's name was Thorvald. It was Freydis who planned this voyage; she hoped to return with a large cargo of timber much in demand back home. She had asked her brother for permission to use his houses, which he granted her. She had then approached Finnbogi and Helgi asking them to make the journey with her for safety. They readily agreed to this for they, too, saw the huge profit to be made on the timber.

Freydis arrived the next day. The two ships had become separated in a storm causing Freydis' ship to fall behind the brother's vessel. Finnbogi's ship was much larger than hers and, carrying a bigger sail, was much faster. Freydis became very angry at seeing the houses already occupied, ordering the brothers out at once. The houses were promised to her and she meant to have them right now. Rather than make matters worse the brothers agreed, moving farther down the beach to build a stone house of their own. This chore along with cutting timber occupied most of the summer months. As winter set in once again, disputes and arguments broke out between the two parties creating ill feelings between everyone.

One morning Freydis awoke before anyone and walked barefoot through the snow to the brother's house. She noticed the door was ajar. Entering she woke Finnbogi and bid him come outside to talk with her. Once outside she spoke to him. "I no longer wish to stay here," she said. "If you intend to stay here for a longer time, I would like to swap ships with you as yours is larger. We can take a bigger load home with us and you will share in the profits when we return." Finnbogi agreed to this. As he and his crew wished to explore this land, they were in no hurry to leave. He thought he could trust her as she was Leif's sister, but unknown to him she was plotting evil at that very moment. She was money hungry and wanted both ships to fill with timber all for herself. Freydis returned to her bed and woke her husband up with her cold feet.

"Where have you been?" he asked.

"I have been to talk with Finnbogi. I tried to buy his ship for our return but he insulted me, treating me very badly. If you were half a man you would stand up for me." Saying this angrily she berated him for being a coward and not defending her. Thorvald, tired of his wife's nagging, woke his men telling them to arm themselves. They went down the beach and surprised Finnbogi and his men while they slept. A fight erupted resulting in all of Thorfinns party being killed. There were five women in the brothers' house that Thorvald refused to kill, so Freydis forced the men to hold the women and then took an ax and killed them all herself. She then gave orders to load the ships; they were leaving as soon as possible. She told all of them to keep quiet about what she had done or she would have them killed also.

Freydis noticed Thorfinn was missing but no matter, he would be stranded here alone and probably die. After the ships were made ready, they boarded the vessels and began the long journey towards home. On the return trip they ran into a strong storm. One man fell overboard, disappearing before anyone could help him; but for this, both ships arrived safely in Greenland. Freydis and Thorvald sold the timber for a good price, telling her brother, Leif, that Finnbogi and Helgi intended to settle in Vinland and that she would make another journey there next year for more timber. It would be quite some time before her evil deed came to light.

Chapter 2

As Freydis made her early morning walk to the cabin and finding the door ajar, she had no way of knowing Thorfinn had awoke early, leaving the house to explore the forest. He left the door ajar so not to wake the others, his good fortune was choosing that day to go exploring.

He left early, packing a little food for a two-day journey. The sun was just breaking the horizon; the mists were rising revealing the blue sky above. He walked to the forest edge where giant spruce and pine greeted him, and he boldly walked into their midst. He carried all his weapons: his stout spear resting on his shoulder, Grasida the grey blade nestled in its scabbard on his back. He was well prepared for whatever might befall him. Dark were the forest depths, the woods seeming to call him ever deeper as he continued on his way. Deer startled as he approached, bounding away through the trees. The sun seldom broke the forest canopy, causing the undergrowth to be sparse. A few ferns with the new growth of fiddleheads unfurled towards the subdued light. The green mosses that grew on the rocks and dead logs were thick and spongy. The trees had gray moss that grew on the north side of their rough bark. The moss rose hung from the high cliffs, their tendrils curling like springs and dripping two and three feet long as they swayed in the gentle breezes. When the wind gave an extra puff, it would blow the petals from the roses and they fluttered to the forest floor like snowflakes. The wild spring flowers swayed like waves in the ocean, some still confined in patches of light snow.

This made Thorfinn's walking much easier. In the distance he heard the thunderous roar of a large bear, a sound he was familiar with from his boyhood in Norway. Many were the times he had hunted with his father listening to the sounds of the forest. He walked all day up hills, down hills, following streams when he could; some of these flowed through gorges sixty to a hundred feet deep. As he reached the top of a tall mountain he paused at the mountain pass turning to gaze at the late afternoon sun low on the horizon in front of him. The mountain foothills to the west seemed bathed in a golden haze, their ridges lived and almost iridescent while their eastern slopes already slept deep in shadows. Above a hawk circled in the clear sky, its wings bronzed by the sun's rays, while far below in a wooded valley a deer and her fawn timidly approached a sheltered pond. Stretching his arms and shoulders Thorfinn shifted Grasida and turned to start down the western slope when a movement caught his eye. Coming up the winding tract was a mother skunk and her liter of babies following close behind, apparently out for the evening meal. Suddenly he realized how tired he was and sat down on a boulder to watch the little family as they sniffed along the trail.

He decided this would be a good a place to camp. He gathered wood and pinecones to start a fire; a few sparks of his flints on the edge of his sword and the fire sprang to life. Having dried fish, wild mushrooms, and a large stem of grapes he settled down for his evening meal. After he satisfied his hunger he prepared his sleeping mat under a large spruce and lay back to enjoy the dark night sky studded with brilliant stars. When he awoke it was a still early morning, the first shafts of the rising sun began to pierce through the tall trees. In this timeless silence he gazed at the treetops, he stretched and felt relaxed after his night's rest. A faint smile on his face, he bounced up, impatient to break camp and start the day's journey.

After he trekked a mile or so all of a sudden his scream shattered the silence. He wavered slightly, an arrow had struck his left arm just below the shoulder. He paled and toppled forward, blood gushing from his wound. As he stumbled toward the cover of the brush he noticed his left shoe was full of blood. Shocked, he eased to the ground and tried to look in the direction the arrow came from. Trying to stifle his groans of pain he held his breath and hoped he was hidden well enough from the foe that decided to put a shaft in his arm. He sat silent, all senses alert and listening for any movement or sound. After what seemed an eternity he now had the painful task of removing the shaft from his arm. He took a deep breath and broke the shaft and pushed the arrow through. The pain was hot and intense causing him to pass out.

When he awoke his arm had stopped bleeding. The pain was severe and unrelenting as he walked. When he reached a small stream he washed and cleaned the wound; the cold water seemed to soothe it. He felt it was time to return to the long houses; he needed some of the medicated powders that were stored there. He began his trip back following the same route he had journeyed in on. He could only guess at who had wounded him. He knew it was a native of this forest but why try to kill him? Thorfinn came across a little cave in a hillside, a perfect spot to spend the night. He gathered some spruce branches to sleep on and lit a small fire to cook his supper. This fire would also keep him warm during the night. After preparing his cave for the night he waded out into the stream spearing a trout and quickly had it on the spit cooking. After this feast he laid back on his mat. As he lay there with his arm behind his head watching the firelight flicker shadows on the cave walls, he remembered the hunting trip with his father when he was younger, especially the time when they were hunting boar in the forests of Norway. It was his first wild boar hunt; he was only five years old. His father spied the tracks of an adult sow and her babies. They tracked all morning until suddenly in the underbrush they heard the snorting and squealing of piglets. Thorfinn ran past his father towards the sounds before his father could stop him. The underbrush parted and out charged a large sow, her beady eyes locked on Thorfinn. He was caught off guard and froze in his tracks. The sow was closing fast, kicking up clods of earth with her cloven hoofs as she rushed toward him. She had two white tusks curling out from her long wrinkled snout; she could rip him in half if she hit her target. Just before she made contact with him he felt his father swoop him up and throw him upon his back. He hung on tightly to his father's neck and shoulders. The sow ripped a jagged piece of flesh from his father's leg before he could kill her with his lance. As he lay there thinking, he remembered his father's fast thinking and bravery, also the scolding he received for running out in front too soon. He vowed to try to imitate his father when he grew up. He also remembered the good pork dinner they enjoyed that night. He convinced his father to let him keep the small piglets he ran down after the dust settled. There were two of them. He tied a grapevine to their legs, and as he and his father made camp in a small cave that night he sneaked the piglets in also.

All was quiet; Thorfinn watched the fire light flicker on the cave walls as he did so long ago. The noisy calls of bluejays woke him from his sleep. The sun rose above the treetops causing the forest to come alive once again. Anxious to be on his way he ate a hasty meal of dried fish and cornmeal, washing it down with cold stream water. He kept his bearings well, a skill he learned from his father during their long walks in the woods. Four days had now passed, as he broke from the woods, walking with a light step towards the houses anxious to tell of all the wonders he had seen. As he approached the houses he sensed something was wrong. Both ships were gone, no one was about, the chimneys were smokeless and the silence was foreboding. He hurried his pace. Turning the corner he discovered all his friends lying where they had fallen in death; the women huddled together in their final moments. Thorfinn was dumbfounded, what could have happened? Most of the men were without their weapons, many killed in their beds before having a chance to defend themselves. He ran to the other houses, empty of humans and provisions alike, everyone and everything was gone. The deathblows dealt his comrades were made by steel weapons, lance and sword; no native stone weapons had created this foul deed. He suspected Freydis right away; she had always been an evil angry woman, so unlike her brother, as the sun and the moon.

Thorfinn stared at the calm ocean waves breaking on the beach, looking into the distance towards Greenland. He was stranded here, for it might be many years before anyone attempted another journey. The crossing was dangerous and few wanted to make it. With a grim set to his jaw he shrugged these thoughts from his mind; there was work to be done. He had to bury all his friends before night fell. There was always the threat of wolves when they caught the scent of death. Thorfinn dug the graves using a wooden shovel and his spear point to pry rocks that made the digging tough.

It was a hard job consuming most of the day, but he finally laid his friends to rest. He then piled rocks on all the graves to protect them against wild animals and erected a cross on each grave for many of these men had just become Christians. They were farmers and traders looking for a new home and meeting an untimely death at the hands of their own comrades. Entering his house he fell into a deep sleep to escape his grief. The next morning he decided his course of action. He gathered the items he could find that might be of use to him: some small amounts of dried fish, cornmeal, everything to make his journey easier. Despite the deep grief he felt over his friends, he turned towards the woods once again with a lighter heart, the forest vastness beckoning him to enter and lose himself in comforting shadows. Thorfinn, more than most men, felt a deep bond and respect for nature. He would put the world of men behind him, a world of hate and killing of which he wished to avoid if possible.

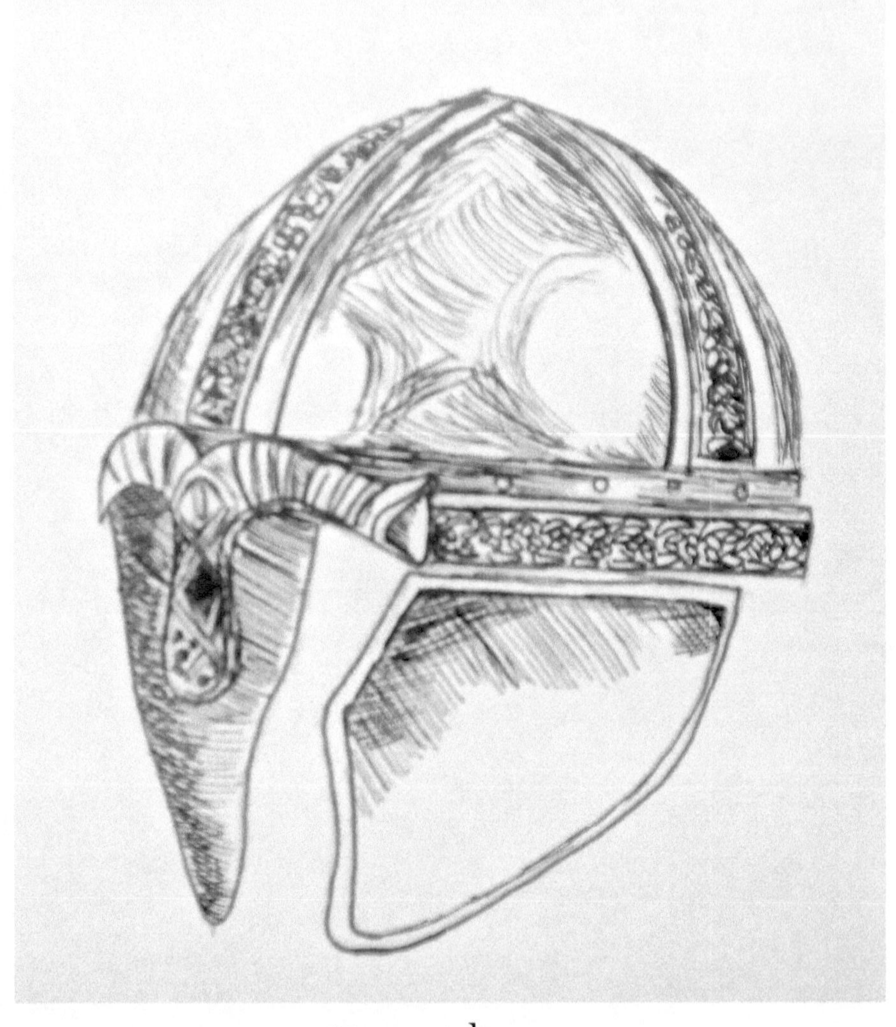

Thorfinn's Helmet

Chapter 3

He turned for a last look at the graves, the house and the sea. He had placed crosses on the graves to honor his friends' memories, a final tribute to all. Many miles separated him from his father's farm in Greenland; he wondered if he would see either again. After some sobering moments in thought, he turned to the forest in earnest.

He followed the same route as on his previous journey reflecting on how things had changed in just a few days. How could Christianity gain a strong acceptance among people unless they changed their warring and killing ways? He had listened to Irish priests visiting Greenland last summer, grasping the words they spoke. The priests told the story of the birth of Jesus, His wondrous teachings for the brotherhood of man. When Thorfinn heard of His cruel death at the hands of the Romans, anger flushed over him. The priests explained to him that Jesus taught forgiveness; He had risen from the dead to ascend into heaven and He had died on the cross to save all men from their sins if they would believe in Him.

Thorfinn was convinced, he had seen what warring, hatred, and killing could do. He made a vow to try and follow the teachings of Jesus and to tell others about it when the chance arose. The teachings of the priest almost convinced him to enter the priesthood himself; their mission to spread the news of man's salvation appealed to his peaceful nature. On the other hand he was young; the call to adventure ran hot in his blood. He would travel and see as much of the world as he could, and then perhaps he could settle down without any regrets. He could then devote himself to the priesthood with all his heart and will. In the meantime he would spread the words of Christ to anyone willing to listen. He would be the bearer of the good news wherever he went. For now he was alone in the wilderness with no one to talk to. How strange the hand of fate could quickly change a man's life. He traveled inland for two weeks, walking west towards the sun. At times he followed streams and rivers climbing often to hilltops to gaze at the country around him, at night he sought out small caves for shelter, gathering spruce limbs for sleeping mats. The streams provided fresh trout for his meals, and fresh berries picked during his walks rounded out his dinner. He found a beehive ripe with sweet honey; this required a lot of nerve to extract the honey and brave getting stung. He grabbed a handful and ran from some very mad bees. One day as he walked on the shore of a calm lake looking for fish he discovered a faint footprint in the sand. It was barely visible. He looked closer. His heart raced a little faster for he realized there were other men in the forest close by. His senses went on alert; from now on he must travel with caution. Tales of natives attacking the first Vikings in the new world were fresh in his mind. He was not afraid but he wanted to be prepared, after all they could be friendly. On he walked, the wind picking up, the gray clouds started gathering and he knew a thunderstorm was on its way. The thunder rolled across the valleys, echoing on its way. The wind swept across the clearings, the grass ahead of it was flattened first by the wind, then by the rain. The combination of shrieking wind and stinging rain caused foxes to huddle deep in their burrows and a herd of deer stampeded madly, pounding this way and that in a frantic hopeless effort to escape. Ahead of the storm, however, the sun continued to bake the rich soil. As the storm front reached the river, the change in temperature became so acute that great streaks of lighting flashed among the dark rolling clouds and explosions of thunder shook the earth below while tremendous updrafts lifted grass and dirt just ahead of the leading edge of the storm.

Taking advantage of these unusual thermals, two birds of prey circled upwards in slow, ever-ascending spirals. Higher and higher they soared, the sun alternately glinting on their wings and outlining them against the lowering thunderheads that seemed to reach out for them. Already they were far above the normal hunting altitude of a hawk and were now approaching their ceiling, beyond which the air became too thin to support them. From that great height not even their honed eyesight could discern the movement of a squirrel.

Down among the trees one pair of azure blue eyes continued to follow the flight of the hawks just ahead of the onrushing storm. Thorfinn had weathered many such storms. He knew that rain would soon drench him and there was precious little to be done about it. He also knew that the storm would pass, the sun would return, and he would be dry again, not much worse for the wear. While the forest creatures scurried about in panic, Thorfinn took pleasure in the joy of the hawks as they soared higher and higher. He wanted to tell people in Greenland how the land was unusually fertile with all the timber and wild animals making for rich pelts, the streams and rivers full of salmon and other fish. The thought of this made his spirits soar.

He knew the valley grass grew lush and ripe enough to support their livestock. The storm reached him, lashed him, drenched him and passed on. The sun came out again and everything looked refreshed. He could smell the evergreen as he walked upon the soft pine needles.

The river he followed stretched along the hills and valleys. When he reached a clearing he squinted at the horizon in the distance. Up above the sky turned a deeper blue than ever, decorated with billowing white clouds. It really was a big blue sky, and at night waiting for sleep to come, lying on the ground he looked up at the stars, which seemed to hang so close that he could reach up and touch them.

Thorfinn's face was deeply tanned, weathered and his eyes seemed to have a superhuman ability to pick out minute details at immense distance. He had been the one to find a spring bubbling happily into small pools of deep clear spring water, its coolness misted the rocks and ferns that scattered around it, the spongy mosses crept over the rocks and lay like different colored patches with hues of greens, aqua, and yellows. The spring frogs jumped with irritation, due to the interruption; the butterflies flitted around the bright colored blooms of the moss roses. He could smell the sweetness of the jasmine vines that climbed high in the trees then descended downward laden with blooms. Thorfinn liked the peacefulness he felt when he listened to the bubbling and trickling of the water as it cascaded over the rocks, trickling down the rivulets into the pools. He knew he was not the first man to enjoy this magical place for he knew there were Indian tribes around.

Constantly on the lookout for more signs he began to climb a high rocky hill to view the countryside. As he neared the top, the area was free from trees and brush caused by lightening fires. As he approached the clearing he heard a loud bellow from a grizzly. He looked back towards the woods, from its shadows emerged a giant grizzly. Stopping and rising to a full ten feet, he sniffed the air for scent. As the bear spied Thorfinn he dropped to his feet charging up the hill, bellowing as he came. His ears were laid back, his nostrils flared and teeth bared and flashing, a ferious sight that would strike fear into any man. Thorfinn turned and ran farther up the hill trying to reach its summit, attempting to distance himself from the charging bear that was rapidly closing on him. He knew he had little chance of outrunning his opponent; a large grizzly was more than a match for one man. Upon reaching the top of the rocky hill he came to an abrupt steep drop off, straight down he saw rapids rushing by at its base. Unable to run any farther he turned and planted his spear against a rock just in time to meet the bears charge head on. The spear penetrated through the animal's body snapping in half. The grizzly made one swipe, slashing Thorfinns shield and arm, knocking him off the cliff's edge. He fell to the water below, head over heels into a deep pool at the cliff's base, the icy hands of death struggling to hold him under. He strained with all his might, the cold water shocking him to his senses as he reached for the surface.

When at last he broke free gasping for air, he was rushed away by the rapids tossing his body from rock to rock. His shield still on his arm, he shook his head to clear his hair from his eyes. He was bleeding profusely. When he thought he could no longer keep himself from drowning he was swept into a large pile of logs and brush. He reached out with one hand and, grabbing on with all the strength he could muster, he pulled and crawled his way to the rivers edge. His sword still hung on his back, his shield on his arm. These were the last things he noticed as he passed into unconscious oblivion.

Chapter 4

As Thorfinn fell a small band of native warriors, men of the forest, hearing the sounds of the struggle emerged from the forests shadows and climbed to the hill's summit. There they found the dead bear with half of Thorfinn's spear protruding from its body. The savages looked in puzzlement and disbelief at Thorfinn's broken spear. As one of them pulled the shaft out, to their wonderment a steel point glimmered in the sunlight. This greatly excited them for they had never seen a steel point before. The savage that pulled the broken spear from the bear uttered a loud shout of surprise. "What is this thing we see, look how it glimmers in the sun light, its edge is sharp like a fine piece of slate. This is not a weapon that we have ever seen before." The man speaking these words was the leader of this small band of hunters; he spoke in the Huron dialect, the language of his people. These men were Huron warriors, hunting for food for their village about one day's journey away. The other men uttered their excitement and interest at the spear demanding to hold it in their hands, each one in his turn.

Their keen eyes took in the signs of the struggle, quickly noticing where a man had slipped and fallen to the river below. This strange hunter must be dead after such a fight and fall, but being intrigued by his spear, they decided to try and find some sign of him. The Huron leader suggested that four of their number begin gutting the bear so they could carry it back to the village, and he would take the others with him to descend and search for this strange hunter.

The Hurons searched down stream when they reached the cliff's base. There was a deep pool here and the current was very strong; the onrushing rapids could have carried the strange hunter away downstream. Their eyes searched the stream's bank missing little. After walking downstream for several miles and finding no sign they forded the river on some huge boulders forming a natural bridge to cross on. If the strange hunter had made it this far through the rapids his body would have been caught on these huge boulders.

Once on the other side they worked their way back upstream until coming upon the pile of trees and brush that enabled Thorfinn to save himself. The Hurons found him lying unconscious where he fell.

The men marveled at this fair-skinned, yellow-haired man and especially his weapons. His sharp ax still in his belt, his wooden shield lay at his side, clawed deep and splintered by the grizzly's claws. On his back the long sword and scabbard still intact waited to be called into service. Surely this man must be a forest demon for no one like him had ever been seen before. With his hands the leader waved towards the woods telling his braves to cut some poles.

Cutting some stout saplings they fashioned a strong litter to carry the stranger back to their village; all must see this man to wonder at who or what he was. The village was half a day's journey away. Packing the bear meat and carrying Thorfinn they set out through the woods. These forest men had to take turns carrying Thorfinn; he was a heavy burden to carry through the dense woods. One man went ahead as they neared the village to gather everyone to come and behold their forest demon. The whole village turned out at their approach, everyone becoming excited as Thorfinn was carried into their midst. He had just regained his senses and beholding all these people he knew not what to think. His arm had stopped bleeding but was mighty sore. The Hurons had laid his shield on his chest as they carried him. When he looked at it he quickly remembered the bear's attack and the struggle that followed.

Was his death eminent? Many were shouting angrily at him and waving their stone clubs in the air. They were afraid of this man, but the elders would decide his fate. The seven warriors who found him now pushed and shoved him towards the tribal elders, anxious to be recognized for finding him. One of the elders touched his yellow hair looking at it curiously. Unknown to Thorfinn he was to run the gauntlet to determine his fate. All the warriors formed two lines. Thorfinn would be made to run between the warriors as they beat, clubbed and sometimes lashed him with bundles of sharp thorns. If he could stay on his feet and make it through the line he might be granted his freedom. This the savages called their gauntlet, and it was their favorite way of testing a new captive.

Thorfinn was pushed to the edge of the screaming braves, whooping and yelling for him to run. The elder waved him on, so summoning all his strength Thorfinn vowed to show them his Viking heritage. He took off running as fast as he could, raising his arms to protect himself as much as he could. The braves struck hard at Thorfinn as he ran. Blow after blow landed hard on every part of his body. The pain of his arm kept his head clear and he rushed onward determined not to go down. He first ran down one side making it hard for those warriors to strike and then running to the other side surprising all. Suddenly he was through the line. Turning he raised a clenched fist in defiance. "Odin," he yelled, reverting to his old Viking god in the heat of the contest. Long would they remember the strength of the north man this day. He didn't know what to expect next. He had survived the gauntlet, but weakened from the loss of blood from his wounds he felt he could not bear much more this day. The savages could easily overpower him to take his life. To his surprise they gathered around him shouting and whooping again, but the expressions on their faces seemed to tell him they were praising him.

The Hurons admired any man who could survive their gauntlet, and killing a grizzly single-handed he must be a mighty warrior indeed. The elders came forward motioning Thorfinn to follow them. He was led to a small bark hut. Food was brought to him and two elderly women washed his arm cleaning it, applying a strong smelling poultice.

He was seated on soft furs covering sweet smelling spruce branches. Everyone left his hut smiling at him; he fell back and instantly went into a deep sleep. His dreams were of his homeland and people he thought never to see again.

Over the next few days he wandered among the village as he willed. The village consisted of about thirty bark huts like the one he slept in. Smoke drifted skyward from each house giving a good smell of burning wood to the air, mingling with the smells of the roasting meat on the spit. Thorfinn walked among the people nodding and smiling. They nodded and smiled as they watched him, still somewhat unsure of who or what he was.

Children played their games happily running through the village. He noticed many women leaving and returning with their baskets full of corn, berries and plants from the forest. Men left and returned bringing fish from the near-by stream. This was a fruitful land with much to offer and these people were skilled at reaping its bounties.

One day a man who seemed different than the others came to him as he sat by his small fire beside his hut. His face was painted half black and the other half yellow. He wore several eagle feathers in his hair and exuded an air of authority and wisdom.

Thorfinn soon learned this was the medicine man, a shaman of the tribe. His name was Lame Duck. He pointed at Thorfinn and raised his eyebrows as if to ask, what is your name or how are you called? Thorfinn guickly grasped what the man was attempting and repeated his name also several times.

"Thorfinn, Thorfinn," he said as he pointed at his chest. This was the beginning of several months of instructions in the Huron tongue. It was difficult and some times exasperating, but he stuck with it with a vengeance. He longed to communicate with these people. There were so many things he wanted to learn about them and their land.

Thorfinn learned there was honesty and reverence for nature among the Huron but they could be cruel indeed to an enemy. He spent the warm summer learning their language among many other things. He watched the men striping large birch trees of their bark and forming it into a canoe. So skillful they were at this art he marveled at the result. A strong, watertight craft perfect for travel on streams, rivers and lakes. As summer faded, the fall winds began to usher in the cold winter breezes. The forest was alive with color as the giant trees shed their leaves in anticipation of the winter to come.

He mended his spear putting the point on a new heavy shaft. The Indians were still fascinated by his weapons, weapons fit for a God. Thorfinn often wondered if any more Viking parties would be coming to the houses on the beach. At times he longed to see his own people again but for now he thought it best to stay here with the Hurons. He learned something new every day and the thing he admired most about them was their closeness and connectivity to nature. The Indian and forest were one and they interacted as if to form one wonderful part of creation.

It was time to move; winter would be upon them soon. The Hurons would move to a sheltered valley a distance of two day's journey for better protection from strong winter winds and snow storms. One day when the time for moving was close Lame Duck brought Thorfinn a necklace of claws, huge sharp bear claws. They were the claws from the bear that Thorfinn had killed as he fell from the cliff. Lame Duck told him the claws would bring him good luck and serve as a sign to others what a mighty hunter he was. From this day forward he would be a member of the bear clan and the bear was to be his totem, a sign of strength and wisdom. Lame Duck placed the necklace over Thorfinn's head and he felt very proud of his new gift. Thorfinn helped pack all things to be of use at the next camp. The bark huts were left as they were; when the snow passed they would return here in the spring once again.

Upon reaching their winter quarters the huts were repaired and made ready for the long, cold months ahead. Soon campfire smokes were drifting lazily skyward once again. Early one morning Lame Duck came to Thorfinn; Thorfinn greeted him warmly for they had become fast friends. "Soon you will be asked for help, if you will give it yellow hair," said Lame Duck. "Our enemies are in our hunting grounds where they know not to come. We must war with them so they will learn to stay in their own lands. If we do not drive them away, our people could suffer hunger this winter for the forest does not supply us during the cold as it does in the summer.

"I will be glad to help," said Thorfinn, but far better it would be if all could live in peace, he thought. The Hurons had saved his life and he owed them much; he could do no less than help when they needed it.

Chapter 5

Early next morning, a light snow was falling gently. With the crisp cold air causing the senses to be heightened in anticipation of the day's journey, he set out with twenty of the strongest warriors known for their bravery in battle.

They were determined not to return until a decisive blow had been struck at their enemies. These invaders had trespassed into their winter hunting grounds and must be taught a stern lesson.

The warriors traveled single file through the woods, staying close to the river running south out of this valley. Two scouts traveled well in advance of the main party to give warning when the enemy was spotted.

Around mid day one of the scouts returned with news; the enemy had been spotted. They had killed several deer and were preparing to carry them away. Thirty men were visible among them--Abanaki braves, the people of the sun, their hereditary enemies.

The Hurons approached cautiously and quietly, Thorfinn in their midst. The warriors crept through the woods without making a sound. It amazed the Northman how quiet they were as all the men took their positions and readied their weapons. The war chief glanced around checking on each man; there was no room for mistakes. The first rush must be strong and decisive, and being out numbered by ten men was not to be taken lightly. Some of the Abanakis were sitting by a fire while others prepared the deer. Thorfinn kept his eye on the war leader ready to attack when the sign was given. When all was ready the war leader let out a whoop and they descended with a rush on the surprised Abanaki. Panic ensued among them; so fierce was the Huron onset. The Abanaki turned to fight, many being killed instantly. Some put up a good fight, as they, too, were strong and proud. A brave ran at Thorfinn with tomahawk raised, yelling as he came. Thorfinn met this rush with his spear, running the man through as he closed with him. All the Abanaki were killed except two; these were let go to spread the word to their village that they were not welcome here and if they returned would be dealt with in a like manner.

Thorfinn's inner conscience told him this was not what the Master of life had meant for his children of the forest. This was the way of the world as it always had been, but he vowed to himself never to kill a human being again unless his life hung on the outcome.

The Hurons returned to their village confident the intruding Abanakis would not return again, for a while at least. Thorfinn spent many months with these people. In fact, almost two full years had passed since he left the beach houses. More and more his heart yearned for his land and his own people. He was learning to paddle a canoe as well as the Indians. He loved learning about woodland lore of which they were masters.

He spent many days walking through the woods with the canoe builders, several men especially skilled at this art. They scouted the woods for the straight and huge birch trees growing in this area, some so big it took four men to reach around them. They would then climb the tree to the height of the canoe they wished to build, slicing through the bark all the way around, then cutting a straight line to its base where they again made a circular cut all around. It was a simple matter to then peel the bark from the tree resulting in a solid sheet of birch bark for their canoe. The Indians used sharp slate cutting knives for this work, Thorfinn's ax proving invaluable, however, in helping them. The men cut ribs and lashings from small cedar trees for its frame, and soon a strong watertight craft, capable of running rapids, striking rocks and carrying heavy loads emerged ready for use. He learned this skill well for someday he might need to build his own canoe.

The Indians also made their paddles from cedar using their slate knives, slender blades that they could dip quickly in and out of the water. He also watched in awe as they decorated the bow and stern with porcupine quills creating a finished product of much beauty. This was an art handed down for generations. In the coming years the white man marveled at this Indian craft. When the Indian paddled his canoe he could see where he was going; when the white man rowed his boats, he could only see where he had been.

Thorfinn could row a boat but it took some time to become skilled as a paddler. Two of the warriors he worked with building a big canoe for large lakes or rivers took him for a ride when it was finished. They launched it in the St. Lawerence River where it was wide and windy. Holding a big piece of bark for a sail they moved across the water at a fast pace surprising the Northman. He learned something that day: why paddle when the wind will do the work for you?

The two braves then let Thorfinn try his hand. He fashioned the gunwales from cedar using the edge of his sword. The Hurons laughed at him, better to use the sharp slate knives, they were much easier to handle. Thorfinn cut a piece of bark from a good straight birch to build a small, ten-foot-long canoe. He did all the work himself, cutting the lashings, gathering the pitch for sealing the seams. The Indians looked on correcting him when he was about to make a mistake. Soon the canoe was finished. It didn't have a dragonhead on the bow but Thorfinn thought it was the most beautiful thing he had ever seen. Now he had to carry it home on a head strap made for portaging. The Hurons slapped him on the back, grunting their approval. They would make a Huron warrior out of him yet.

Chapter 6

In the summer of his second year with the people he asked the elders permission to take a wife. He was content among the Huron but also lonely. He needed someone to share his thoughts and desires with, someone to bear his son or daughter which he hoped to have someday. A small war party returned with several captives. One of these was a very beautiful woman, an Abanaki, hereditary enemy of the Huron. She was dragged into the village by a rope around her neck, as were the other captives, her head held high with pride. She meant to show no fear to her captives; if she were to die she would meet her fate with courage. The woodland people were taught from birth to accept their fate without showing fear if ever their enemies captured them.

Thorfinn admired her courage, the defiant look in her eyes; she had the strength of a Viking, he thought. He talked to the elders inquiring what her fate would be. He learned she would be adopted into the tribe because of her youth and strength. Hanaka, the main elder of the tribe, explained to him what her fate could be. "She is young and strong, yellow hair. She can be adopted into our tribe if she will accept it. Sometimes these Abanakis are so proud they prefer death instead. Thorfinn was told many tribes adopted captives in this way to increase the tribe's strength. Even warriors were adopted if they showed exceptional bravery. If, however, she tried to flee she would be killed.

Thorfinn asked her name. It was Wildflower, she was as beautiful as a star shining in the evening sky he thought. "If I may, this is the woman I would take to wife, if she will have me," he said. The elders suggested he take her and beat her good if she displeased him but this he would not do. Either she stayed of her own accord, or she would be free for another.

Wildflower was amazed at seeing Thorfinn's fair skin, yellow hair, and blue eyes. She had never seen these things before. She knew if she was to survive she must give in to her captors' wishes; better this than a slow cruel death in the fires. She would bide her time for now until the chance for escape presented itself. When it came, she would flee through the woods like a deer back to her own people. Pushing aside her initial fears she went with him as she was told, resolved to do her best to please him. She soon learned Thorfinn was a kind and gentle man who liked to laugh with her and who treated her kindly. Thorfinn was a good hunter; he also was learning many things from the Huron. Wildflower was never lacking meat for her table, and to her surprise Thorfinn even helped her prepare it. He was skilled at catching salmon that were plentiful in the streams and rivers, big salmon, larger than any he had ever seen in Greenland. Many were smoked and dried for sparse times in the winter months. These were happy times. The whole village was busy preparing food. The smokes from many campfires drifted lazily skyward. Wildflower was happy and content.

This man was different from the Indian braves. As the months passed she found a deep affection for him, blessing the day she had been captured to become his. One day as they walked along a special spot in the forest that they both enjoyed she told him of the child that was coming--his child. Thorfinn was filled with joy when he heard this; a son, hopefully, that he could teach and share everything he knew, part Viking and part Indian. What a glorious combination. He was very happy. And should it be a girl instead of a boy, she would be beautiful like her mother, brave like her father. God was good granting him this bounty.

Thorfinn was granted the son he wanted so badly. He was a healthy baby boy with blue eyes and a head full of coal black hair like his mother. They named him Thor, after the gentle god of the Vikings, he of the blue eyes, he would grow to be wise and strong, a leader of his people. For now he was a small baby and had to grow, as only time will permit. Thorfinn and Wildflower were well pleased and happy with their lives now. At this time Thorfinn began telling the story of Jesus around the night fires.

Perhaps some day a savior such as Jesus would come to unite all the forest people in peace, perhaps Jesus himself. A legend started to grow, passed by word of mouth all around the land creating hope in people's hearts. The legend of a messiah that would unite all forest dwellers in peace.

The Huron tribe that Thorfinn and Wildflower lived with desired to return to their hunting grounds of old across the big lake, the land of their fathers. This was a long journey of many miles; it would take him farther and farther from his houses on that far away beach. If he and Wildflower went with the people now, he knew he would probably never see his own kind again. He was content here in the forest, but he wrestled with the decision about what to do. Wildflower told him she would follow him anywhere; it was his choice to make. He spoke with Lame Duck inquiring where the tribe meant to go. Lame Duck told him, "If you wish to visit your own kind again that is good. You should follow your heart in all things. Someday if you wish to join us again, you have but to follow the big river west until you reach the rapids. It is a long distance. Then you must travel north to a big mountain; it will call to you with its beauty. There you will find us in the land of our fathers. We have been gone too long; it is time for us to return.

Thorfinn thanked him for his kindness. "You will be in my thoughts and heart forever, my friend. May your journey go well. Look for my return for I believe fate will draw me back to you again. I will take my wife and child and return to the stone houses on the beach. I doubt if anyone will be there but I must try. I fear if I go with you now, I will never make the long journey back. It is very hard to turn away from your own people. The Huron are my brothers and I love the forest, but still I must try."

Lame Duck understood telling Thorfinn he would always be welcome should he desire to return someday. "Until then, stay safe, my brother." Saying this he turned and faded into the wilderness.

Chapter 7

Thorfinn could wait no longer; he had to make a journey back to the beach houses to see if any of his people had returned. He told Wildflower of his plan. Even though she was somewhat afraid, she agreed to go with him. They bid goodbye to the tribe and entered the forest returning the way he had come years before. They journeyed many weeks over mountains and streams. When they came to the rocky cliff where he fought the bear he showed it to Wildflower. He could not believe he had survived such a fall; it was a long way down to the bottom of the cliff. All went well for them, the weather was good and the forest provided all their needs. One day as they came to the top of a small hill they smelled the salt sea breezes, spying the ocean at last. Unbeknown to Thorfinn he had emerged somewhat west of the houses, but the area looked familiar; he knew he could find them.

As they left the forest walking along the gravely beach they could see in the distance a large number of native warriors attacking someone...Vikings like Thorfinn? Their ship was pulled up on the beach and they had taken cover by it. They were greatly outnumbered; they needed help. Hiding his wife and child in the forest close by the beach he charged with a savage yell towards the Indians unleashing his sword, the blade glinting in the sunlight as if it was on fire. This filled them with fear as they had heard of the yellow-haired giant of the Hurons. Fearing the Hurons to be with him they turned and ran into the forest with all the haste they could muster. Thorfinn approached the men by the ship. One was a man he knew very well, Thorvald, brother to Leif the Lucky. He had been shot in the armpit with an arrow and knew he would soon die. Thorvald asked Thorfinn and his men to bury him here on this point of land, a place which thereafter would be called cross point. Once again Thorfinn felt deep grief over a death of one of his people. He greeted the other men, some of which he knew and was very glad to see them. He told them what had happened years ago at Leif's houses on the beach. The men knew of Freydis and her husband's evil deed. Rumors had got out until Leif learned the truth, banishing her from living close to anyone ever again; she would be an outcast the rest of her life.

Thorfinn determined to help his fellows repair the keel of their ship and longed to return to Greenland with them. Wildflower said she would follow wherever his heart led him. The next morning feeling younger than he had in years, he rolled up his sleeves and got to work. He had the rare ability to make quick bold decisions that often turned the tide of battle. He often marveled at the miracle of God's handiwork in nature and man.

He wanted to go back to Greenland with a load of timber, furs, pelts, and grapes; he also wanted to build a farm for himself and his family so his son could get a good education from the Irish priests. He promised himself he would succeed in this. God forbid if he failed, he could end up working in the livery stables or tenant farming someone else's farm with his wife's help.

He felt sad leaving his son's birthplace and his wife's native home. He vowed then he would return someday, but for now he felt they should challenge their son's quick and inquiring mind.

Now he was becoming restless; it was October and chilly as he turned for his favorite high stand of trees fired a brilliant red and gold in the early morning sun. Entering the forest he knew he would have to set sail soon. He needed time alone to think things through before the trip.

Finally to his astonishment he noted that the long shadows of the trees now lay in the opposite direction. He had been up there the entire day making his plans to return to Greenland working as he thought. He descended the hill finding that his mind had become wonderfully quiet and peaceful. He also felt his appetite beginning to gnaw at his stomach. He tried out the little flute he had carved for his son while he rested at mid-day. He began to play and sing some old Norse songs from his homeland.

This was the first time in his life that his heart felt so full of joy, but it was only a precursor of what would transpire that evening.

When he returned home, the chores being done and his appetite satisfied, he settled down by the fire with Wildflower to tell her of his dreams and enjoy the warmth of the crackling fire. Then Wildflower told him of the new baby on the way. He grabbed Thor holding him high over his head, telling him he was about to have a new brother or sister, and he praised God for his good fortune.

The next morning dawn came quietly. The mist rose off the water, songbirds greeted the sun and squirrels scolded one another. It would take about two more weeks of hard work to load the ship; the furs and pelts would be loaded last. They would take plenty of dried fish, salmon, berries and grapes; they even had some smoked bear meat. As he and the men were loading logs onto the ship, one that was being hoisted off the ground swung out of control hitting Thorfinn in the mouth, busting his lips and breaking one of his front teeth. The pain was intense; he was spitting blood and seeing stars. Wildflower came running with a cloth and a big mug of seawater to rinse his mouth out. He suffered miserably with swollen gums and pain for weeks; only his will got him through the days of pain.

Finally the day to leave was upon them, they made ready in haste, rowing the small boat to the ship with the last load. They got under way but there was little room left after the timber and furs were stored. The ship was seventy-six feet long, seventeen and one-half feet wide by six and one-half feet deep. The pine deck boards were loose so that the timber could be stored. The ship's skeleton was made of oak timber from Norway; the strakes were joined together by round-headed iron rivets driven through from the outside and secured inside by means of small square iron plates. The caulking was of tarred animal hair or wool. The hull was kept in shape by nineteen frames and cross beams. The strakes, or ribs, below the waterline were tied to the frames with spruce root lashings, a device which contributed much to the ships flexibility.

With her mighty keel and flexible frame and planking the Viking ship was an inspired combination of strength and elasticity, and this power to cross seas and oceans did not exhaust her excellence as a raider. A shallow draught, rarely exceeding three and a half feet, allowed her to penetrate all save the shallowest rivers, gave her majesty of harbourless shelving beaches, and facilitated the rapid disembarkation of men at the point of attack. By turning into the wind and making off by oar she was almost immune from pursuit. The sixteen pairs of oars were of pine so regulated in length that they struck the water in unison. The mast, too, was of pine, about thirty-five feet tall with a big square sail made of heavy woolen cloth, strengthened by a rope network and hoisted on a yard some thirty-seven feet long. She had a gilded dragonhead and tail and strengthed prow and gunwales. The winter weather did not lend itself so well to travel by sea but this ship could handle almost any kind of weather. The Vikings were seamen skilled as no others. As their ships crashed through the rough waves they gained strength and thrilled at conquering the angry sea's challenge. Many believed Odin or Thor guided their craft, protecting them from harm.

Thorfinn watched the forest disappear in the distance with mixed emotions but turning his face to the sea drank in the wonderful salt air, the ocean breezes that were so much a part of him. Wildflower did not know what to think about this ship and these men like her husband. She had never set eyes on the ocean before and now to be flying over the waves was almost too much to understand. She put her trust in her Northman, hoping to see dry land once again. Thorfinn had a repetitive tooth ache so severe that it robbed him of sleep and ultimately tormented him so much that he finally pulled it from his jaw with his forefinger and thumb. He was happy to escape the pain so severe and unrelenting it might have caused another man to wish for death. As it was he overcame this throbbing pain by the sheer strength of his indomitable will. He hoped the inflammation connected with it would soon subside. He knew to rinse his mouth with seawater; this his father taught him long ago. The voyage to Greenland had been safe so far, even with the gales and deadly sea fog they had encountered. All of a sudden Thorfinn's heart leaped with joy. They found themselves in the midst of seals; this meant they were close to the coast. He sent a man aloof as a lookout. A snappy breeze was blowing from the west with the promise of more wind behind it, and to the leeward appeared and disappeared a black speck. As they got closer they could see the mountains topped with snow, the glaciers running down their sides. As they neared the calm cove in front of them they lowered the sail and struck the oars, stroking long and hard to reach the shore. When they made anchor they lowered the small boat taking Wildflower and Thor to shore first. She was glad to be on dry land again, the trip over was terrifying and her stomach was unsettled all the way.

To Thorfinns surprise and gladness his old friend Leif was standing on the shore to greet them. He had been informed by the villagers of a ship anchoring in the cove. Leif offered them his house to stay the winter in and sent word for his wife to set three more places for supper. Leif had his big wooden-wheeled cart with his favorite team of Fjord horses, so they loaded up and headed for the warmth of a good fire. Leif introduced his wife to Wildflower; she had a kind face and jolly personality. Supper was already on the fire pit, the smells were delicious: home-baked bread and a hardy stew of caribou meat, and after eating dried fish and berries on the voyage this was a real feast.

Leif the Lucky had welcomed Thorfinn and his family warmly. His father, Erik the Red, had been close friends with Thorfinn's father. They had sailed on many an adventure and summer-time raids of which the Vikings were well known and feared. But that was in the past, things were changing now. There was more a search for peace and a gentler way of life. Thorfinn anxiously told his tale of life with the Indians, of his wife and son, and the rich bountiful land he had lived in. Leif thought long and hard on whether to make another journey or not, but finally decided to stay on his farm as it had expanded greatly and took all his time to tend it.

He told Thorfinn if he ever wanted to return to the new lands, he would give him a ship and crew to make the journey. In the meantime, he would give him land to farm here if he desired it, land to farm and raise his son.

He knew not if others would attempt the journey, as people seemed to be settling down more and abandoning the old ways. Thorfinn thanked him for his kindness, saying he would spend the winter here and then decide what he would do. He was still a restless soul and the call of adventure was calling him even now. His son was growing quickly and he showed his father's strength running rough and tumble everywhere.

The family decided to stay in Greenland for now to let Thor grow and learn the Viking ways. The days were long and dreary, the gray clouds of winter scurried across the windy sky. The sod roof began to drip rainwater in several places as Wildfire began the evening meal. The fire stoked early that morning was just right for cooking on; the coals glowed bright orange and gave off blue licks of fire. She was baking ground corn bread and caribou stew mixed with home-grown onions, carrots and potatoes. She also put in some rutabagas for seasoning.

The cabin was warm and the simmering stew filled the air with mouth-watering flavors. As she bent over to remove the large kettle with the stone ground corn bread in it she felt a searing pain radiate from her back to the front of her. She knew the time was near for the baby to arrive. She promised her friend, Gudrid, who lived about a mile away, at the first sign of labor she would send Thorfinn to fetch her. She pushed the kettle of stew towards the back of the fireplace to keep it warm; it was almost done for it had bubbled for about three hours.

She called Thorfinn from the doorway; he came running with an armload of wood. She told him it was time to fetch Gudrid. Thorfinn left at a run, it would not take him long for the one-mile trip. Thor helped his mother start a kettle of hot water and prepare the bed. She spread out all the soft hides and quilts she had, resting ever so often as the labor pains were coming closer now; Thorfinn and Gudrid should be coming any moment now. By the time they arrived she was doubling over with pain; she lay back on the bed, stifling back the scream that filled her throat. Gudrid was a heavy-set woman with long braided hair that she wrapped around her head. She had a happy motherly face and was soft spoken and jolly. She had assisted many times in birthing. Wildflower was relieved that she was there.

Thorfinn waited in the other room with Thor. He stirred the good smelling stew and buttered some corn bread for the two of them. They might as well have their supper for it might take a while for the baby to arrive. He was grumpy and a bit nervous, getting up to tend the fire and empty the pans of water from the leaks dripping here and there from the sod ceiling. He kept walking and pacing, looking out the window then back to the door that was covered with a blanket that separated it from the kitchen. He heard the moans and groans from the other room. He kept calling out, "Is everything O.K.?" Gudrid would answer back, "She's doing fine, won't be much longer." Finally Wildflower gave a shrill scream and then he heard a soft mewing sound that became stronger. Gudrid wrapped the girl child in a warm woolen shawl and gave her to Wildflower. She peeked in to survey the baby from her tiny nose down to her rosy toes. Finally they yelled for Thorfinn and Thor to come and greet the newest member of their family. The baby was healthy and good-natured, pretty as a misty morn. As Thorfinn thought about her the name Misty Dawn came to mind. He said it over and over and told Wildflower he thought this would be a good name. Wildflower agreed. As Misty Dawn grew older, she became more beautiful; her rich raven black hair, azure blue eyes complimented her high cheekbones and high carriage. Her hair grew down to the middle of her back. She could be feisty at times like her mother and strong like her father.

During this time, He of the blue eyes, brother of Misty Dawn, learned many things: Viking legends, farming with his father, and seafaring.

Whenever Thorfinn made a voyage to trade Thor went along too, learning the ways of the sea. Wildflower did her part also, teaching him the ways of the Indian. He was equally proud of both sides of his ancestry, and he walked with his head held high ready to be a friend to any man he met.

Two years later, two priests came on a longship from Ireland one summer. They had come to help people understand the new religion of Christianity. Most had accepted the new religion but some still clung to the old ways. Thorfinn was extremely interested in their teachings. He helped them build a small church, plain and simple but beautiful still with its ornate carvings, white washed in the sun. There was one window in the front, a round window with a beautiful piece of stained glass brought by the priests from Ireland. The priests spent two summers on Greenland. During the cold winter months when they could not visit farms to talk with people they welcomed anyone, anytime to spend time at the church to learn.

Thorfinn took his son there every chance he could. Thor was now ten years old, almost eleven. He was growing straight and tall like his father; he, too, was lithe and muscular. There was no mistaking his Indian heritage. If not for his blue eyes he resembled a son of the forest more than a Viking. Thor had an unquenchable thirst for knowledge, bothering the priests constantly to teach him about the world.

He studied their words in earnest for he, too, thought someday to teach the woodland people of God--a belief in one God that loved all mankind as equal.

Thorfinn and his family spent two more years on their farm. Thor was now thirteen years of age. Thorfinn decided to return to Vinland and find the Huron. Wildflower missed her green forest and lakes also just as Thorfinn had missed his people. When Thor heard they were going back he eagerly awaited the time to go.

Thorfinn asked Leif for a ship as he had promised and Leif was quick to give it to him, a large longship that would carry much timber from the new world if they should ever return. Leif handpicked a good, eager crew to man the ship, thirty trusted men, and men Thorfinn could rely on. One of the men was named Karlsefni. With his wife, Gudrid, they hoped to settle in Vinland and farm. They took a large bull and two cows along to start their farm.

They put to sea in early spring when the ice broke up; a long journey like this was much safer in the spring than winter. Thor could not remember the voyage to Greenland years ago, he was just a baby then, but now he rode the bow as the ship dipped and rose from wave to wave. Much to their delight they sailed through a large pod of whales slapping their tails on the surface as they dove, blowing water twenty feet into the air as they broke the surface. Dangerous as this was it was also very exciting. Now, too, was a good time to learn the skills of reading the compass; too many mistakes and you were off course. With a good steady wind and moderate seas they held steady on their course. Thor also helped Karlsefni take care of his cattle. Not many of the other men wanted to help with this, as it was not a pleasant job.

Then one day clear and bright they spotted land. Thor was the first to see it. Now they were home to the forest again.

Chapter 8

The Viking ship moved through the calm clear water towards shore. Men lowered the sail slowing its approach. With the sail secured each man took firm hold of an oar rowing in unison, singing a hearty Viking song learned from their fathers. The song helped to keep each man's oars striking the water together. Thorfinn stood at the stern guiding the ship towards shore.

Thor stood on the bow along with Karlsefni and Gudrid, all three staring at the dark green forest stretching as far as the eye could see in front of them. Even Karlsefni, who had come from Norway, was impressed. A virgin forest with all its wealth lay before them.

As the ship gently ground to a halt in the shallow water, the crew lowered a small boat. Gudrid, Wildflower and Misty were the first to go ashore, and then followed Thor, Karlsefni, and Thorfinn. Gudrid could not wait; she had to inspect the stone houses. She and Wildflower ran excitedly up the beach, with Misty hot on their heels, to get a closer look while Thor just ran everywhere looking at everything at once. His father smiled to himself and was pleased. He knew how his son felt; he had felt the same years before on his first voyage here. He showed the stone graves to Karlsefni and reflected back to the time he had buried his comrades years ago. "This was a sad time for me, my friend; I wasn't sure what happened but I suspected Freydis. She was an angry evil woman from the first moment she arrived here. How she could be the sister of Leif is beyond me. At least he learned the truth about her finally."

"No one could believe what she did," replied Karlsefni. "She brought great shame on herself but she is paying the price now." The two men walked back down the beach to the ship. Before the men could rest the cattle had to be unloaded, a large bull and two cows. A ramp was lowered into the shallows and the cattle smelling the fresh green grass ran down the ramp towards shore. They were allowed to run free, as they were too interested in eating grass to wander far.

Karlsefni then joined Gudrid to look the houses over. Some repairs would be needed to the roofs and a few stones replaced in the chimneys, but by and large the houses were still in good shape. "I will make this house warm and cozy for you, Gudrid, then maybe you'll cook me some good food, eh?" At this he laughed his loud boisterous laugh as only he could.

All this work could wait until tomorrow, however. Tonight a big fire would be lit on the beach; a feast to celebrate their safe arrival would be enjoyed by all. The strong Viking ale on board ship would be passed around for all to enjoy. This was a joyful time; two good people would try to settle here to build a farm, the first permanent Viking settlement in Vinland. Thorfinn almost wished he was staying to help them but he longed to find the tribe, his tribe, once again.

The next day Thorfinn, Karlsefni, and the men set to cutting roof poles, peeling sod from the ground to repair the roofs and gathering stones for the chimneys. It would not take these men long to make the houses sound and sturdy, ready for the elements to do their worst.

Karlsefni also cut poles for a cattle pen to hold them secure when necessary. His big bull was his pride and joy. With this bull he would build up his little herd and do his plowing too. "When you return here again, Thorfinn, you will see a farm to make your eyes dazzle."

Thorfinn looked at his friend and smiled. "If anyone can succeed here it will be you, my friend. Just take care and be on guard; there are men here in the forest and it is not known if they are truly peaceful or warlike." The two men walked towards the cattle that were munching grass peacefully and content. Thorfinn stayed around helping for several days but as things took shape, having imparted all he could to Karlsefni about the land and forest, it was time to start his journey. Karlsefni called for another feast to send Thorfinn and his family on their way. Fresh venison roasted on an open fire along with more ale, which proved to be a fitting meal to say goodbye over. Wildflower and Gudrid had become fast friends. Now that they were to part each shed some tears.

The next morning they rose early each carrying a caribou hide packed with supplies. Carrying his weapons he bid Karlsefni and Gudrid another more somber goodbye. Waving a last farewell the family headed towards the woods, disappearing into its dark shadows and quickly losing sight of the beach houses and their friends.

The family hit the forest following a game trail along the river, west-southwest, those were Lame Duck's words. Thorfinn planed to build a long canoe, fit for the river, as soon as they found some big birch trees. It was time to teach Thor this skill anyway. As they made their way through the woods about three day's journey from the beach houses, Karlsefni and his men were approached by a large group of warriors. At first they wanted to trade for iron weapons but when Karlsefni refused the Indians became angry and attacked, killing several of the Vikings right off. Karlsefni and his crew fought back killing many braves as Gudrid ran to the cattle pen, turning the bull loose she swatted him on his rump sending him straight for the Indians. The sight of the bull with his big horns put them in a panic causing them to flee to the woods to escape.

Karlsefni and Gudrid decided it would be too dangerous to stay here now having lost several men in the battle. If the Indians returned in force they might not be able to defend themselves next time, better to return to Greenland and then to Iceland. They could still cut a load of timber for the return trip and use the profits for a new farm. The cattle would be turned loose to roam, as it was very difficult to transport them by sea. Gudrid was with child also which she bore in the coming days. They named him Snorri, the first Viking baby born in the new world. This was another good reason to leave now; they couldn't risk their child's life against the savages.

But all this was unknown to Thorfinn and his family as they made their way through the giant spruce forest. They traveled on following the river until coming upon a large stand of birch trees. Thorfinn halted here to build his canoe. There were many miles ahead to travel; using a canoe would be much easier than walking. Thor found a tall huge birch, straight and true. Climbing up it he cut all around its top, and then making a slice straight to the tree's base he cut around the tree again. Thorfinn peeled the bark away from the tree thus having a perfect piece of birch, good for a twenty footer. Next came the job of cutting the ribs, gunwales and lashings from cedar trees nearby. In two day's time the craft was ready for a test run.

Thorfinn made three paddles with his ax and knife, and then launching the canoe he and Thor both paddled it with pride. Not a leak anywhere, and the craft flew across the water. Loading all their gear they struck out downriver. When the winds blew Thor put up his bark sail making them fairly fly across the water.

For several weeks they paddled west camping at night. The weather was good and there were plenty of fish for the taking. As they neared the big rapids the river narrowed. They had passed the high cliffs where the city of Quebec would rise someday under the French. When they could travel no farther Thorfinn and Thor pulled the canoe well up on shore, finding a good place to hide it they covered it with brush, hiding it so skillfully even Wildflower's sharp eyes could not spot it.

They shouldered their packs again and headed north. The big mountain was visible to the north, several days walking lay ahead of them through thick forest. The little family had to travel easy now for Wildflower was with child again. A fairly large fast-flowing stream running its course from the north to empty itself in the rapids proved to be the best route for them to follow. They would have water and fish for their meals and the route would be easier walking by the stream. At times they came upon beaver ponds where the beavers working hard slapped their tails on the water's surface. Thorfinn also spied a mother moose with two young calves munching grass in the shallow water. Thor was too young when he left the woods to remember all these wondrous things but he soaked it up now. Wildflower showed him various plants used for medicine, she taught him the difference between good and bad mushrooms, and how to make poultices for wounds. Thor listened intently for he meant to learn all the woodland lore and learn it well. There was more wildlife here than in Greenland; he loved seeing the moose with her calves. They were not afraid either, just giving them a parting glance as they walked by. The forest was alive; each step might bring some new wondrous thing and adventure. The stream splashed and cascaded over numerous small waterfalls creating a music all its own. They were on a well-worn path now, a warrior's path leading from the river north to many inland villages. Perhaps they would see their own tribe soon.

Chapter 9

Thorfinn, Wildflower, Misty and Thor headed farther into the woods; fall was approaching and the forest was alive with color. The trees would soon be shedding their leaves, but for now the forest was ablaze. The gold, oranges, purples, and bronze leaves were lived this time of the year. The going was easy and the little family made good time, and in the evening after setting up camp they built a nice fire to cook the fresh trout Thorfinn caught from the stream they were following.

Thor was a tall lad now, coal black hair and a ruddy complexion, but his blue eyes were a sure sign of his Viking heritage. He constantly asked his mother and father many questions some of which they could not answer. He wanted to know who made the stars, the forest, seas and all the creatures in them? He had heard many answers from many people but it was a constant amazement to him. Nature made him question and wonder at every turn.

As they walked on their way one day about midday they came upon some faint moccasin tracts by the stream bank. They hoped it would be their people and they must be close for tracks to be so easy to find. They continued to follow the stream and as it widened they came upon a small valley. In the distance they could see smoke rising from many bark houses;

they were home at last. Lame Duck stepped out of the woods with a huge grin on his face; he had been watching them approach for some time. Thorfinn grabbed him lifting him off the ground. "My brother, you still live. I thought never to see you again."

"Or I you," Lame Duck replied. "I see the boy turns into a man and his mother still walks as proud as ever and you also have another little one. You have been a busy man indeed."

They walked on to the village; fall leaves crackling beneath their feet and a musty scent from the forest floor waifing over them. Soon winter would be upon them again. The village greeted them with exuberance, much clapping and dancing and all the people seemed happy that the Northman had returned again. A huge feast would follow that evening, for this was a great occasion.

Many years had passed, some of the old ones had departed their life on this earth, but most still lived and were well and content. Thorfinn knew he had to start building a cabin before winter set in. He did not want to burden anyone else about where his family would live. Everyone pitched in to help him; this was the way of the woodland people. A stout frame of poles covered with bark soon was erected. Sleeping mats and warm skins were furnished for all. Now all that was needed would be a supply of dried meat and fish along with some corn to see them through. Wildflower intended to gather some wild berries and it was time for Thor to go on a hunt. Perhaps he and his father would be lucky enough to take a large buck; the meat and hide would serve them well. Thor had been practicing with the bow and arrow of which the Huron were very adept. He was learning well, he could almost do as well as his father and was proud of it.

Thorfinn, Thor and two of his new friends left the village early in the morning, walking silently through the woods on deep beds of pine needles, every sense on alert for the deer, their eager eyes darting to every movement, every sound. They reached a thick area of under brush where they could conceal themselves and wait. They all sat down laying their bows across their laps and remained motionless and silent. The forest was also silent due to their arrival but after a short time the forest came alive again as the squirrels, birds and other animals decided it was safe to resume their daily lives. Thorfinn had learned to stalk and hunt as well as any Huron, but it was Thor who spotted a large buck feeding in a clearing not far ahead. Fitting a shaft to his bow he took aim and released the arrow which flew straight to its target. Straight to the buck's heart it flew and the hunters as if one man all pursued him into the brush.

The deer was soon found having given in to the arrow in his side. The hunters thanked the Master of life for providing this meat, and then they thanked the deer for his life. They only killed what was necessary to sustain their lives and they gave great reverence for the animals they killed for food. The work of gutting the carcass befell them and they hurried to get it done. The full moon was on the rise when Thorfinn hoisted the deer onto his shoulders to begin the long walk back to the village. They followed a dry creek bed back for it was easier to see than walking in the dark forest. When the moon was hidden they could barely make out the sandy path in front of them. The two Huron braves had slipped back into the woods in hopes of seeing another deer on their return journey but Thorfinn and Thor stuck to the creek bed. Darker it became but the creek bed gave some outline of their way be it ever so dim. If they had to traverse the woods right now, pitch-blackness would envelope them.

Thorfinn walked cautiously carrying the heavy carcass. Thor was but a few steps behind him when all of a sudden Thorfinn disappeared from sight. Thor froze in his tracks calling out to his father, "What happened, where are you?" he cried out.

Thorfinn was busy spiting sand out of his mouth and couldn't answer for a moment; he had stepped over the edge of a small waterfall or where one would have been if the creek were running water. He fell about ten feet with the deer landing on top of him. Finally he responded, "I am all right, son. Stay where you are, I will come back up to get you. Luckily I landed in the sand and not on a rock." Showing Thor a way around the drop he hoisted the deer on his shoulders once again and with the moon coming out from behind the clouds they could see well enough to make it home. A feast ensued for all the next day; when Thorfinn had meat he shared it happily with the rest of the tribe.

Wildflower was with child again and with spring approaching it was time to take their long walks in the forest, which they both enjoyed so much. As the two of them walked in the forest, gentle breezes blowing through the spruce trees brought them close to nature and the creator that fashioned it. Thorfinn was truly happy now. He was back in his beloved forest; no more would he yearn to return to his native land. This was his home and these were his people. He was blessed with a wonderful wife to share it with and soon another child would be born.

The baby came early one morning as Thorfinn and Wildflower walked together not far from the village, there was no time to return to their hut; this baby refused to wait for ideal surroundings so Wildflower hurriedly veered from the path into the undergrowth. The mists were still heavy and swirling all around, the forest was just coming alive with the sounds of its creatures as Wildflower gathered a stack of pine needles. The labor pains were coming stronger now. She lifted her fringed skirt to her waist. Doubled over in a squatting position on the fresh needles she grabbed a limb of a half fallen tree for she knew the time was near. Groaning in the last stage of her labor she agonized in the pain. Breathing fast and hard she took one last gulp of breath and pushed as hard as she could; the baby made its entrance into the world. The baby was a beautiful baby girl of perfect proportions and evidently a good set of lungs due to the loud cry of discomfort she felt from the rude awaking of being born. Her eyes were swollen shut, her skin was very red, and she had a head of thick black hair. After an overall check by her mother she was placed in a small soft otter pelt which her mother had been wearing over her shoulders. The baby snuggled deep in the soft fur and quieted her cries for the moment. Thorfinn had been watching and waiting nervously close by, his weapons in hand to protect her if need be. Having a baby was a very natural thing for a daughter of the forest but danger was always close by in the woods. Wildflower stepped from the forest and handed the baby girl to Thorfinn. He looked down at her lying in his huge hands. She wrapped her little hand around his finger and held on tight. He was amazed and delighted at her strength; they decided to name her Idun after the Norse god of spring.

"She has your blue eyes, husband, but I hope she won't wander like you," Wildflower said laughing.

"We will teach her to stay at home," he grinned. Slowly they made their way back to the village to share their joy with everyone.

Chapter 10

The summer passed as winter storms set in with a vengeance, bitter cold biting winds, snowdrifts piled deep. It was a time of quiet and retreat from the weather. When one did venture out to hunt, snowshoes had to be used; no one could walk without them. The small band of Hurons of which Thorfinn and his family were a part had prepared themselves well. Foodstuffs aplenty were stored for the long months ahead; the strong bark huts with their fire pits in the middle were warm and secure. Let the winter roar outside, this was a time to relax around the fires telling tales and listening to stories from the old ones. The Huron's huts were constructed by setting poles in the ground and bending them over to make a strong framework that was then covered with slabs of white birch bark laid and overlapped to shed the rain and snow. At the very top was a smoke hole about one foot square; three round stones about four inches high were placed in a triangle atop the last layer of birch bark, on top of these stones a thin slab of slate was placed allowing the smoke to escape and keeping the rain out. They also built their sweat lodges and long meetinghouses this way. The long meeting houses were about fifty to sixty feet long and twenty feet wide, they had three or four fire pits down the center with resting mats built up off the dirt floor all along the walls. Here they gathered in groups from the winter's blast, they loved to tell tales and talk of goblins, witches, and lost souls. The children loved these times: it was a time of learning, new experiences, and a time of heightened emotions including anticipation, anxiety, disbelief, fear, surprise and wonder. To the Indian mind the forest was a magic and mystical place; this is why Thorfinn was thought to be a forest demon when found by the Hurons years ago. After the last meal of the day the Indian warriors began to gather in the long house with their clay pipes; these were held in great veneration. They were usually wrapped in fur and entrusted to a special custodian. The forest warrior took great pride in his pipe. Many were decorated with carved designs of birds or animals along with beads, porcupine quills, and feathers. The women neither used or cultivated tobacco, it belonged entirely to a man's world, being planted and weeded by the warriors themselves.

The men would enter and be seated around the fires to smoke and tell their stories of past experiences to the rest of the tribe. It was warm and the firelight made the inside of the long house glow orange like a lit pumpkin. The people would sit on the spruce mats, wrapping their warm deer hides around them. As the aromas of the spruce branches mingled with the smoky smell of the fires everyone became soothed and content. Men tended the fires adding fuel as necessary, as the fires grew higher and hotter the shadows on the walls became bigger and danced faster. Outside the wind moaned and the wolves howled as the snowflakes fluttered to the ground. Sometimes the tree limbs would scratch against the bark hut causing the people to shrink away in fear. The moon was full, the night was bright with its magic, and this night was the right night to relate some of their ghost stories. When all the people had gathered in the long house, the Great Spirit and Master of life was thanked for past favors and humbly besought to give health, peace, and contentment to all mankind. Then came the great feather dance with its prayer of thanksgiving, it being one of the most beautiful of the Huron rituals. After this each started his story. The Huron lived in a haunted world in which the dead walked forever along with a world of supernatural monsters.

Mysticism and imaginative power were outstanding in the Huron personality. To them ghosts were everywhere. Black demons were as plentiful as black bears, witches tormented and thwarted the red warrior, the night was filled with ferocious monsters out of the minds shadowy past especially on misty, rainy, and cold winter nights in the forest. A warrior arose and began telling his story, he had fallen into a deep trance for days and when he walked among the living again he told of the monstrous serpent that lived in the deep river that rose to the surface and tipped his canoe over and dragged him down into the deep depths. He struggled with the monster slashing with his sharp flint knife until he gained his freedom breaking to the surface and upon reaching the lakes shore thanked the Master of life for being spared from the monster. Each warrior in his turn did likewise until late into the night, people gradually leaving to go to their own huts and sleeping mats.

The wintertime was also used to make new snowshoes, replenish weapons and prepare hides for clothing. Snowshoes were made of grape vines woven over a form of spruce branches. These were needed very often for the winter snows came often and deep. A man could make little progress through the snow without snowshoes on his feet. New bows and arrows were also on the list; the warriors were experts at creating straight smooth shafts with expertly made points. The arrowheads had to be struck and shaped by hand along with their knives and spear points. One fun thing to do during this winter time would be to make flutes and teach their children to play them. All these things had to be learned from a young age to prepare the child to survive as an adult and teach the next generation, thus keeping the tribal traditions alive. When the people gathered in the long houses they also listened to the medicine man telling the story of creation by the Great Spirit.

At this time anyone wanting to talk or ask questions were welcome to do so.

Thorfinn took good advantage of these times to explain his new religion. If the people could not accept this he felt sure the one God of all mankind could send a messiah of their own people to unite the woodlands in peace.

He tried to make the young hotheaded braves understand a life for a life was not the way to live. Their was plenty here in the forest for all. When warfare ceased all the tribes would prosper.

When weather permitted the men would hunt and fish, cutting holes in the ice, using a strong grass braided line to catch fish. Thor was becoming a warrior of superior skills; he was a master of guiding a canoe through rapids and fast-moving streams; where his foot trod in the forest no sound could be heard. He never failed to return from a hunt without some game. The first deer he felled was a medium-sized, two-point buck. He was not allowed any help skinning it for this was the true test of what he had been taught by listening and watching his father. The first thing he did was sharpen a round pole about three feet long. This he stuck through the deer's hamstring on one rear leg then lifting it around the middle with head down he raised it up to a large branch of a tree. Placing the other sharpened end over the branch he stuck it through the other hamstring thus the deer hung head down from the tree branch with his legs spread apart. The next thing to do was to bleed the deer so as not to spoil the meat. He then started at the center of the underbelly and cut down towards the head. As he did so the entrails came falling out, the heat of the freshly killed deer meeting the cold wind caused steam to rise through the air. Thor reached in and pulled the rest of the entrails out being careful not to rupture the bladder for urine would contaminate the meat. He cut it out in one piece and placed it on top of the rest of the entrails in a small hole he prepared on the spot where he was performing this task, this was left for the wild animals. Thorfinn stood by looking on with approval as Thor worked at the skinning. The lad then carried water from the stream nearby in a hide pouch to wash the inside of the deer. When this was done Thor hoisted the animal on his shoulders for the walk back to the village. A man must be able to carry his own kill out of the woods if he was to gain the respect of other hunters. Thorfinn's family always had more than they needed, sharing often with others, for each kill they thanked the animal for its life and also thanked the Master of life for granting them this food for their survival.

Thor's close friend was a young warrior named Grey Owl. He loved to hear Thor's stories of the Vikings and strange lands; things hard to believe but he knew Thor's word was true. He was a woodland warrior, his life had been spent in the forest, but this was soon to change….

As summer approached two Indian runners from a village farther up the St. Lawrence entered their camp proclaiming excitedly the news of a strange craft on the river. It was a huge ship with a ferocious dragonhead on its bow. These runners knew of Thorfinn the Northman. Believing them to be some of his people they hurried here to tell him. The ship was moving slowly down river towards the rapids. Thorfinn thanked the men for their trouble and presented them with an iron ax head for each; no finer gift could he have given them.

Father and son prepared to set out, their hearts pounding with excitement. Several days of fast travel would see them at the rapids. Here they hoped to find the ship and the men of Greenland. How had these Vikings been able to travel so far west? They were an adventures bunch for sure. These men would have news of Greenland but most important they could answer the question of why they were here. Thorfinn was quite a bit older than Thor but he was still very strong. He kept up with his son running through the forest, jumping anything in the way. Father and son laughed at their competition as the time and miles flew by. They were forced to stop at night, the woods becoming pitch black making travel impossible. Whenever the moon came out in all its glory lighting the forest floor as if it was day, they traveled on. Beef jerky and handfuls of corn supplied their needs, eating on the run most of the time.

One black night as they rested by the same stream they had followed on their journey to find the tribe they lit a small fire for comfort. Thorfinn speared a large pike for their supper, a sharpened stick serving for a spear. He was carrying only his sword and ax so he could travel fast; Thor had his bow, he thought to shoot some fish but his father beat him to it. As they sat talking, resting from their day's run, wolves could be heard calling their woeful cries from the dark forest. Thor threw some more wood on the fire causing it to blaze higher. A strong fire was the best defense against a wolf. One of them would sleep while the other kept watch. As the morning sun worked its way through the thick forest canopy they rose and promptly set off again. They were fast approaching the river now, soon they would see the men and their dragon ship, at least they hoped so.

Chapter 11

They saw the ship anchored by the rapids; it could travel no farther. The men on board were Vikings for sure, young men who had known Thor as a boy in Greenland. Remembering Thor's stories told over and over as a boy and wanting to be like him, upon growing old enough they, too, managed a ship to make the journey. One of the lads was closely related to Leif the Lucky; this proved a big help in their acquiring a ship. They didn't really expect to find Thor but the journey was worth the danger if only to view the new world. Upon entering the big river they just continued west ready for whatever came their way. As they sailed down the river approaching some high cliffs many small canoes full of savages set out from shore. As they neared the longship they fired their arrows, which the Vikings easily avoided behind their shields. The wind was with the Vikings and they soon outdistanced the Indians. This was the only incident of seeing any trouble with the woodland warriors on their entire journey down the river. When they did lose the wind they rowed until the huge sail filled with the wind again. Now to have actually found Thorfinn and Thor was good fortune indeed.

All the men spent the night around the fires celebrating their reunion, telling tales of home, the Vikings listening to stories of the forest. Thorfinn learned Karlsefni and Gudrid had returned to Iceland and was saddened over the fact that their desire to settle had been ruined by the savages. Providence seemed to rule out any of his people making their homes here. More and more he felt he would be the only Northman of this new world.

The young men expressed a desire to push farther on; the huge lake at the rapids end seemed to call to them. They asked Thor if he would journey with them. He spoke many native tongues now and could help them greatly. Thor jumped at this, asking his father's advice. Thorfinn told him he could journey if he desired; he would not hold him back. The men asked Thorfinn to help them move the ship past the rapids. He agreed to help although he did not wish to see his son leave.

Thorfinn asked his son to return to the village and bring back all the men who could be spared, and to also bid goodbye to his mother and explain what they were about to do. While Thor returned to the village he had the young Vikings cut trees, straight and true to make rollers to move the ship on. They would pull the empty ship out of the water with ropes, placing the ship on the rollers. Once on the rollers, with many men pulling, some pushing with poles, they could move it down the beach. While some men cut trees and skinned them for rollers, others unloaded the ship carrying most of the goods down the beach to the point where they meant to re-enter the lake. All the men broke out in song as they worked, songs their fathers had sung as they sailed over the seas. No man ever had a more adventurous heart than a Viking. Centuries of sea faring, wandering, and raiding had instilled this in their blood.

Thor hurried through the woods to his village where he met Grey Owl heading for his hut. He carried his walking stick made from the trunk of a tall pine tree. It had a black rattle made from the shell of a turtle. As he glided along the path leading to the village the spring breeze felt good against his skin. He was glad the long winter season was over. At its best it was a season of irritation and monotony, when hunter and warrior must pass long days without adventure amidst the squalling of children and the complaints of women. Thor came running to him explaining what he was about to do. Grey Owl thought about going with Thor and the more he thought on it the more it appealed to him. Thor entered the village calling all the warriors together. With Grey Owl's help he convinced them to come with him and help. With approval from the elders they prepared to set out. A handful of warriors were left behind to protect the village but the rest were eager to go.

Thor went to his mother's cabin telling her what he was about to do, explaining all about the ship, the Vikings and the big adventure ahead of them. Wildflower was afraid in her heart, afraid she would never see him again. But knowing him to be his father's son she bit her tongue and held him tight feeling the strong body and amazing bigness of him. He was a kind and loving soul and he loved his mother; she felt this as they clasped each other close. Tears sprang to her eyes despite her efforts not to let them flow; a lump came to her throat as she said a short prayer. Oh Great Spirit, please keep him safe and healthy on this stretch of life that he is about to enter. She then removed a small leather pouch from around her neck and placed it over Tho's head. It contained a round smooth stone believed by her to be a good luck token. Thor kissed her goodbye, hugging little Misty and Idun. "When I return they will be all grown up, I expect. Tell them of me. I will return with enough tales to last a lifetime." Saying this he hugged his mother once again and removing the eagle feather from his hair he handed it to his mother saying, "Keep this for me until I return for I will return with the Great Spirit's help." He turned and left his mother's hut seeking out Grey Owl and the many warriors gathering in the center of the village. Each man carried enough corn and jerky to sustain him on the voyage to the river.

Joining the warriors he set out with Grey Owl by his side. "You might wish to join us, my brother," Thor told him. "My friends will welcome you and I would be honored." Grey Owl thought on this as they moved through the forest. Perhaps he would go after all.

Chapter 12

Thor and Grey Owl, along with most of the village's warriors, a large force indeed, set off through the forest at a fast clip. It would take several days of fast travel to reach the rapids. Some men had brought corn and jerky to eat on the trail but small game had to be hunted and prepared to keep the men's strength up.

Thorfinn and the Vikings had finished cutting the roller poles; they were ready to pull the ship out of the water as soon as Thor returned with the village's warriors.

Everything on the ship had been unloaded and either carried downstream or placed on the beach. Even the huge sail with its rigging had been removed making the ship much lighter.

When Thor arrived Thorfinn gathered everyone around him explaining what had to be done. Tonight they would feast on venison; tomorrow they would go to work. Grey Owl and the warriors looked at the young Vikings armed with their swords and sharp axes. These Vikings were a fearful bunch but easy to like, the young men from Greenland welcoming the Hurons. The gifts they could give they put in front of the Hurons to their delight--knives, axheads, and spear points, all things that made the Huron happy.

The next morning the men tied ropes to the ship, using pulleys from the rigging tied to trees. On Thorfinn's word Viking and Huron alike pulled and strained, some men using poles for leverage. Everyone gave their all in the effort. The ship moved slowly at first; then, under everyone's effort, it began rolling easier. It was not an easy job but it was working.

The Vikings broke into song again; the Hurons too began to clamor. You couldn't call it singing but it unified the Hurons' efforts. Probably many an animal or bird looked on that day wondering where all these men came from destroying the serenity of the forest.

The ship reached the lake and being pulled into the water was soon floating free once again, its proud dragonhead facing west towards the unknown. Another day was required to load the ship, putting the sail back in place. Everyone let out a cheer as the sail unfurled, the giant red cross shining in the sunlight.

The work was completed. The Hurons were thanked again, most of them fading into the forest for the journey home. Many a warrior had a new ax or knife, a treasure to guard with one's life. Several of Thorfinn's good friends stayed to make the return journey with him.

Grey Owl told Thor he would like to go with him. This was great news; his experience in the woods would serve them well. Thorfinn told the young Vikings their journey would have to wait about two weeks if they wanted Thor to journey with them. The great new year festival was about to begin, and it was the major event of the tribe's year. It began on the fifth day of the second new moon after the winter solstice. This moon, called Diagona or the long moon, first appeared at the end of January or early in February. The festival was held in the central longhouse of the village and Thor along with Grey Owl did not want to miss it. But in order to leave with the Vikings, they would.

Only occasional rumors of tribes to the west had reached these forests along with tales of other large lakes and a giant waterfall between two lakes. There was no way of knowing what might lie before them. Thorfinn bid his son goodbye, telling him to take care, to be wary of strange tribes; many people were peaceful but many others desired war more than peace.

Chapter 13

Thorfinn returned through the forest with a saddened heart. He wondered if he would ever see Thor again, there would be many dangers facing them but he knew his son to be strong and resourceful. He had never hid from life's dangers and he wouldn't want his son to either. He and Lame Duck walked together; there was no need for hurry now.

Lame Duck spoke, "I have heard many rumors of a new war chief to the north. He has been talking war among his people. Those northern Huron have long resented us due to ancient hatreds between our fathers. I hope nothing comes of it but it would be well to prepare."

Thorfinn mused the words over in his mind; war once again, would there never be peace among these people of the forest. "Perhaps the tribe would be better off to leave this area, find a new home far away," he replied. Lame Duck told him, "They will have to drive us away. Our fathers are buried here. We will not leave unless forced.

Thorfinn knew what was coming in the future. It would take many more wars and killing until people would turn to someone to unite them. The small group continued on their way, the main party from the village having already passed this way on their return. The men followed the stream north again, a well-used path winding through the woods close by.

Water cascaded over boulders and rocks, worn smooth by eons of rushing waters. After winter thaws this stream turned into a raging torrent for several months. Piles of dead trees thrown and caught by rocks and trees on the banks testified to its force.

Whenever one traveled in the forest it was a habit to go as quietly as one could even in peaceful times. At any time small war parties out for glory and honor could attack.

There were three other men with Thorfinn and Lame Duck, walking somewhat in front of them; a whoop sounded from the forest as an arrow struck the lead brave killing him instantly. Another whoop and yells resounding from the woods brought several northern Hurons rushing from the woods, war clubs raised ready to strike a killing blow.

Thorfinn pulled Grasida from her scabbard killing one warrior as he sprang from a boulder straight down on Thorfinn. The sword thrust penetrated his body clean through, Thorfinn's mighty arms wielding the deadly power in an instant. He pulled his ax from his belt and threw it full force at another about to strike Lame Duck. As quickly as it began, it was over, the sounds of two or three crashing through the woods was a welcome sound to Thorfinn.

Lame Duck grabbed Thorfinn's hand thanking him for his life. "If not for you I would be walking with my fathers now. Their rush was quick. This is a bad sign to find these men are roaming this far south."

The dead brave was a good friend of all of them. He had no family but was liked by all. Thorfinn cut some poles for a litter. They would carry the warrior back to the village where he could be buried with honor. He would be placed on a burial platform along side of the other members of his long-gone family. This man had died because he came to help with the ship…a woodland warrior skilled in life in the forest struck down for no reason.

It wasn't long before they reached the village. Many grieved for their slain comrade. He had been known for helping anyone who needed help.

His body was prepared in his best deerskins, weapons laid by his side. Wrapped in several large hides, he was carried to the burial grounds where his body was laid on a platform high in the air. Many of his friends threw ashes over their heads as they sang a song of death for their friend.

Thorfinn warned the village to beware, keep a sharp watch; enemy warriors stalked their lands and could strike any time. He posted a group of warriors to traverse the forest close by; their sharp eyes would have to give warning if an enemy approached.

Chapter 14

By now it was late summer and early fall crept closer once again. Everyone set about gathering and storing food for the long winter.

Thorfinn wished to kill another bear. The warm fur would keep them warm during the cold months ahead, and the meat would benefit many. Being a small band, everyone helped each other to survive. If one brave was fortunate to do well hunting, he shared with those less fortunate than himself.

A large grizzly was spotted circling the fields while the women were gathering corn one day. Sometimes these bears came dangerously close to the village creating problems for everyone. Most of the time the camp dogs would scare them off with their barking but this did not always work. The women froze in their tracks as the bear stood on his hind legs sniffing the air, being downwind of them he didn't catch their scent and ambled away in the opposite direction. After what seemed eons of time the women headed back to the village to tell Thorfinn and Lame Duck. The two men decided to track the bear and take him if they could. If this bear was injured in any way he could turn into a real problem with the potential to harm someone. With the help of a stout bow Thorfinn thought he would have a better chance than years before during his first encounter.

Thorfinn and Lame Duck packed some food, gathered their weapons and headed north to where the bear was seen last. The forest was thick here; a man could walk all day and never see the sun breaking through the forest canopy. The two hunters heard a fast flowing stream cascading over boulders not far ahead of them, knowing the bear would stay close to water they made for it, spreading out with a distance of about one hundred feet between them. Even this short distance made it hard for them to see each other. A few shrill birdcalls from each man allowed him to have some idea where the other was.

Alert eyes pierced the forest gloom, ears listened carefully for every sound. As they approached a small hill Thorfinn came upon a large tree with long claw marks at least ten feet off the ground. This was a huge grizzly they hunted. The claw marks were fresh, and there were fresh droppings on the ground. Now they had to be extra careful. If this bear came upon them before their weapons could be readied it could go bad for them.

In anticipation the men proceeded cautiously. Thorfinn fitted a shaft to his bow and Lame Duck did likewise. Just ahead of them a clearing created by fires and windstorms drew their attention. Their eyes scanned the clearing and the forest edge. Lame Duck entered the clearing ahead of Thorfinn. As he did the grizzly came charging out of the brush nearby. The bear had been stalking them all along. Lame Duck turned, raising his bow to loose his shaft but the bear was upon him breaking small trees and brush. As he came ears laid back, growling and frothing at the mouth, teeth flashing ferociously, Lame Duck thought he was a dead man. Thorfinn pulled his bow to its fullest and took deliberate aim. He had but one chance. The arrow left the bow striking the bear dead center killing him instantly. The bear fell on Lame Duck knocking him to the ground. Thorfinn rushed to his side, helping him up. His only injury was some claw marks on his chest, made as the bear fell on him. Lame Duck had been lucky indeed and was once again grateful to Thorfinn for saving his life.

Darkness was fast approaching so they decided to make good use of this clearing. They dragged and pulled the bear to its center, and then after gathering some brush struck flint for a fire. They would be compelled to spend the night here and carry the bear out in the morning. They expected visitors during the night; wolves would soon arrive. The scent of bear and man drifted through the trees calling to them. They gutted the bear burying the remains so as to lesson the scent but this would only help for a little while. They cut a stout sapling to carry the bear's carcass. This would be an arduous task retracing their way back through the thick forest.

Shortly after dark as the men squatted by their fire, gleaming eyes could be seen on the clearing's edge. The wolves were circling all around the clearing, working up their courage to charge. If not for the fire they would be upon the men and bear meat in a flash. All that was needed was one reckless charge to set them off. The men threw more branches on the fire causing it to burn higher and brighter. Thorfinn threw blazing pine cones with glistening sparks of pitch at the gleaming eyes, hoping to keep the wolves at bay. Thorfinn had his spear in hand, the best weapon that he could use if they charged. Lame Duck shot his arrows at several believing he hit one, but due to the darkness most went amiss.

All of a sudden from the forest edge a huge gray wolf charged straight toward them. Thorfinn gripped his heavy spear and planted his feet. He caught the wolf in mid air as it tried to jump the fire towards them. Catching it on the point of his spear he hurled the wolf over his head back towards the forest's edge. At the sound of the crying screams of the fallen animal, the others seemed to lose heart and soon no more eyes were visible in the darkness. The rest of the night, however, saw each man taking turns at small snatches of sleep.

The next morning as the sun rose in the heavens the two hunters set to work skinning the wolf for its warm hide. Hoisting the bear up by its carrying pole to their shoulders they set out for the village. The going was slow as they knew it would be, but at day's end they entered the village. Many tales were told around the fires that night as the whole village feasted on bear meat. Much praise was heaped on the hunters and Wildflower looked eagerly forward to having a warm bearskin blanket for the cold nights ahead.

Chapter 15

Winter came and went once again. Springtime saw little Misty Dawn growing bigger each day. Thorfinn wondered how his son, Grey Owl, and the young Vikings were doing, wishing them well in his thoughts, wondering where they might be, what adventures had befallen them--perhaps this summer would see their return. In the following month rumors and tales of the northern Hurons, a much larger and stronger tribe to the north, began drifting into the smaller tribes of the south concentrated on the northern shore of Lake Ontario. Alarming news of war parties roaming through the woods attacking small villages, burning crops and killing all they came in contact with. A new war leader had come to power--Stone Bear--the same man Thorfinn had met years before when they were both young at the battle of cross point where his friend Thorvald had lost his life.

Now he was on the warpath again determined to drive the southern Huron tribes out of Ontario across the rapids never to return. This animosity between the northern and southern tribes had age-old roots, old hatreds that most could not even remember but they existed still. Thorfinn was alarmed over this news. He knew his small tribe could not withstand the onslaught headed their way. They, too, would be overwhelmed and destroyed if they did nothing. Conferring with Lame Duck and the elders they decided the best course of action to take if they were to save the people.

A war council was convened one night. A large fire burning in the center of the village, each warrior struck the war post with his tomahawk in turn, and all had a chance to speak, voicing his opinion. Almost every man elected to follow Thorfinn whatever his decision would be, whether war or fleeing the enemy to safety. There were many women and children to think of.

Thorfinn rose when all were finished. Wildflower had made him a new white deerskin shirt of which he was very proud. He wore it now with Grasida resting on his back ready for service. "My people, I came to you years ago. I am now one of you in heart, mind and soul. My thoughts tell me for all the peoples' good we should flee this land as soon as possible. I know the warriors want to fight, but I fear we will be utterly destroyed if we choose this way. If you will follow me I will lead you south across the rapids into the dismal wilderness. There our enemy will not follow. We and many others like us must find new lands, for I fear we will never be able to return here again."

All the tribe listened in silence knowing Thorfinn was right. Lame Duck rose now and spoke to the tribe. "Gather all that you can carry; we leave at dawn's light. Thorfinn and the warriors will guard our retreat. We must move through the forest as fast as possible, so take only what is necessary. Go now and make ready." The warriors retreated to their huts to prepare for battle; each man prepared his paint, applying it in a somber fashion, preparing their minds for battle. They were fleeing but should the enemy catch them they would fight to the death. Some were painted solid black or yellow, others used many colors, each with his own design used by his father and father's father before him. Even Thorfinn painted his face half blue in the tradition of the Celts. A Christian he might be, but the old ways were still with him especially when it was time for war.

This was a small village boasting at the most forty warriors but they were brave to a man. Thorfinn called the warriors together. Drawing Grasida from its scabbard he drew a half circle in the dirt explaining how they would protect the fleeing village. The first sign of an enemy the call of the whippoorwill was to be sounded drawing them all together. The sun was just breaking the horizon as Lame Duck hurried the people on their way. The village would be burned but there was nothing to be done about that. Women and elders urged the children on entering the deep forest following the stream south towards the rapids. Lame Duck caught up to Wildflower and Misty. "Stay close by me so I can defend you if necessary. Your man is in the rear and may be unable to find you if we are attacked."

"We will stay close old friend," she replied looking anxiously back to the forest behind them. After half a day she looked back to see smoke rising above the tree tops. The village was burning. Their enemies would be fast approaching now. They must try to travel faster. Everyone became more alarmed sensing the closeness of their pursuers. Finally the tribe broke out of the forest; the rapids were in front of them. Lame Duck hurried them across. The rocks were slippery and the rapids rushed around them making the crossing difficult. Soon all were across except the warriors and Thorfinn. Whoops and barbarous yells sounded from the forest. Thorfinn appeared urging the warriors to cross and protect the people on the other side. Several warriors crossed and waited behind large boulders at the waters edge, their bows ready. If the enemy tried to cross here he would feel their sting. Thorfinn was still on the other side about to cross when Stone Bear broke from the woods, his head and upper body painted black with a yellow flash from his head down across his chest. Stone Bear's warriors stopped at the forest edge. The Huron chief brandished his warclub taunting Thorfinn to turn and fight him in single combat. Thorfinn pulled Grasida from its scabbard. If he could kill Stone Bear now, their enemies might not pursue them any farther.

Thorfinn stood at the water's edge, his sword in hand waiting for Stone Bear's charge. The Huron chief let out his most ferocious yell. Brandishing his club above his head he charged across the clearing, a look of hate and fury in his eyes. Thorfinn clenched his jaw and prepared himself, looking dead on at his enemy. Stone Bear let out a blood-curdling yell, raising his club high for the deathblow. Thorfinn sidestepped his opponent, driving his sword deep into his chest. The look of surprise on Stone Bear's face would stick in Thorfinn's memory forever. The Huron fell dead at his feet. Wildflower yelled, "Thorfinn, Thorfinn hurry across before they are upon you, hurry."

Thorfinn turned casting a glance at the woods. She was right, the Huron warriors were emerging from the forest still not believing their chief was dead. Thorfinn jumped from rock to rock crossing the rapids to safety. All his braves retreated to the woods to protect the people ready to fight if the enemy tried to cross. The northern Hurons paused at the water's edge yelling and waving their weapons. Thorfinn and Lame Duck watched, hopeful that this would be the end of it. There was no way for them now but south into the dismal wilderness and the unknown

Chapter 16

Thorfinn and Lame Duck led their people to the shores of a large lake stretching southward as far as the eye could see. Travel would be easier for all if they followed its shore, far better than traveling the mountains. "I will climb to the top of that mountain just ahead. From its top I will be able to see just how far this lake extends toward the south if I am lucky. Perhaps I will not see the end of it even then," Thorfinn exclaimed.

He left the people resting on the lakes shore, regaining their strength; they desperately needed the rest after the trying time they had just encountered. Warriors stayed alert in case the northern Hurons tried to follow but this was doubtful. A long, hard journey lay before them if they were truly to be safe from their enemies. On this day the weather was made for climbing; cool and tranquil amid the green shadows of the giant hemlock, beech and yellow birch groves at the foot of the mountain. After about forty-five minutes of steep ascent through the lower and middle forest zones the trail suddenly leveled off, skirted around a small cliff and then leapt sharply upward. Thorfinn had to scramble for handholds and toeholds but shortly the trail led to a dazzling promontory, a charmed opening revealing a long valley below. He continued upward through evergreen, birch and poplar until reaching the top he could see nearly a hundred miles down the long blue lake. This is where he would lead the people. The country to the south looked promising, rolling green hills and blue water. There they would build a new village. He descended the mountain and returned with his good news; two week's journey would see them to their new lands. That night around the campfires the elders spoke of taking a new name for their tribe; no longer would they call themselves Huron. They had been disgraced and warred on by their own kind. From this day forward they would be called Onodagas, people of the hill. Many other small tribes were forced out of the north by the Hurons and they too adopted new names for themselves: Mohawks the flint people, Oneida, Cayouga and Seneca. But it would be several years before all these tribes made contact with each other. Far to the east lived the people of the sun, the Abanaki, the people of Wildflower before she was captured. She was Onodaga now and would be for the rest of her life.

Thorfinn spoke often at tribal meetings to tell all who would listen about his hope for peace among all the forest tribes. If they would have faith in the Master of life he was sure to send a messiah to unite all people in a great time of peace. He would heal the hatred in men's hearts and all would live in harmony with God and nature as they were meant to.

Thorfinn preached peace but in his heart he knew it would be long and hard in coming. Talk of peace was good but he knew they must be prepared for war. He spoke to the elder of his idea to build a strong log palisade around the village. "We will sharpen points on stout trees and bury the other end in the ground. If we can do this like I plan, our village will have a strong defense against any who wish to make war on us." All the men worked hard at this task, it required many trees and a lot of digging but soon a strong palisaded wall weaved it self around the camp. There was only one entrance which could be easily defended against an enemy; watchful sentries peered into the forest from each corner always on alert. They would not run again. This was their new home and they meant to defend it to the death if need be.

In the following year the people prepared the ground for their crops, the soil was rich and black. Corn squash and pumpkins grew before their eyes; the woods were full of game, and the lake supplied them with all the fish they could eat. Occasionally small bands of Mohawks and Abanakis tried to raid their village but the palisaded walls kept the village safe. If enemy warriors were captured, their lives were spared if they accepted adoption into the Onodaga tribe, thus increasing their overall strength.

Misty Dawn grew bigger every day, growing to a beautiful young woman. She had her father's spirit and was wise beyond her years, a daughter of the forest skilled in woodland lore. Her mother taught her all the medicines, how to find them and what to use them for; in this art she had no equal. Her beauty caused Thorfinn and Wildflower some concern, as many young braves seemed to visit them quite often of late. One day soon they would lose her to a husband but this was inevitable and a natural part of nature. Idun was approaching twelve years of age. She was different from most children her age, spending many hours with animals in the forest observing them all day long. For the last several years Thorfinn and Wildflower had noticed her close bond and the ease she had around animals. She had no fear of animals and they seemed to sense this, responding to her, calm and unafraid. Thorfinn recognized this gift. He had heard of it from the old Irish priests. She had the gift to form a special bond and communicate with animals of the forest. All the forest people had a high respect for animals but this was something special.

Little Idun walked through the woods all day long by herself seeking out nature and all its creatures. She walked by a stream watching the trout darting in the clear water. Suddenly she heard a low whimpering coming from a thicket. She paused motionless, eyes and ears attuned to the movement in the thicket, There it was again--a low whimpering painful sound. Creeping closer she parted the branches and peered in. There lying next to a large spruce was a young wolf pup. His shoulder was laid open and bloody, he had several other cuts and scrapes. The center pad of his left foot was slit all the way across and laid open. As she peered in she locked eyes with the wolf pup he starred motionlessly into her eyes with fright. She began talking to him in soft soothing tones. He seemed to be soothed by the sound of her voice He relaxed his ears and lowered his head and accepted her touch on his paw. She continued to pet him and talk in soft tones. She went to the stream and dipped her scarf into the water and returned to the pup and began to wipe some of the blood from his fur, she wrapped the scarf around the wound on his paw. She ran back to the village to seek help in getting the pup back so she could care for him. She feared the village people might not like the idea of the pup being in the village. She sought out her father and using her pleading voice told him of the pup and asked him for help getting the pup back to the village. Her father stated the wolf was a wild animal and might be too much to handle when he was healed. "Please, father, let me try. He let me pet him and his foot looks so bad. Maybe mother could put some of her Indian magic on him. And when he is healed if he wants to leave we will turn him loose. Please father lets help him."

"All right, Idun, but understand I will have to be the judge of the danger involved." Thorfinn followed her to the thicket and the pup was still there. Idun spoke soothing words to the pup while Thorfinn made a small litter. They carefully lifted the pup onto the litter without any resistance; it seemed to sense they were trying to help. Back to the village they went. As they reached the gate of the village the villagers gathered around curious of the small ball of fur, several warriors uttered their displeasure of a wolf being brought into the camp. Thorfinn told them he would be in charge of the pup. Idun knew she could tame him to be her friend and companion if given half a chance. Her father made a small shelter in back of the hut to provide shelter to protect him and let his wounds heal. Idun and Wild flower went in to the forest to gather herbs and mosses to make a poultice. Wildflower knew this would be a lesson to teach Idun again about the magic of the forest medicine as she taught Misty Dawn many moons ago. After gathering the herbs they hurried back to the village. Then Wildflower ground the plants and herbs together. In applying them she then put a layer of moss and bound them with thin grape vines. The poultice would have to be changed in two days. Until then the pup would have to be kept quiet and given fresh water and food. This was Idun's job.

The wolf raised his head locking his eyes on Idun once again. As she looked at him she could feel the bond between them growing ever stronger. She would name him Skoll after the Norse wolf that chased the sun. He would be by her side to chase away the enemies of her people. In the following weeks mother and daughter tended to the wolf. He was healing well. Idun brought him food and water and sat by his side for many hours at a time. The wolf regained his strength and rose up on his feet one morning. Thorfinn watched from a distance, his bow in hand, not knowing how the creature would react now that he had regained his strength. Skoll walked to Idun and raised his paw, which she took in hand. He licked her hand as she held his paw, no words were spoken, only their eyes talked to each other. Idun then led him out of the village into the forest. This would be the real test. If he wanted to return to the wild now would be his chance; if he chose to stay with her, she would be overjoyed.

They entered the dark forest depths. The wolf's senses came alert to the forest sounds. Idun stroked his neck and talked softly to him. In the distance she heard another wolf utter his cry. Skoll's ears perked up hearing it also. He looked in the direction of the cry and looked back at

Idun. Two or three times he looked at her and back to the cry of the other wolf. Seeming to make up his mind he came to her and licked her hand. She was happier than she had ever been, grabbing him around his neck for a big hug. He was hers to run through the woods together, to share her special places, to be her friend. From that moment on girl and wolf were always together. She soon became known as the wolf girl and would one day become a legend among the Onodagas.

Many stories were told of this half Viking, half Indian girl and the wolf that never left her side. Many times she came to the aid of people working in the fields when a wild animal threatened them. Skoll even attacked an Abanaki warrior trying to kidnap a woman working on the edge of the cornfield close to the forest. To the warrior's surprise he was suddenly met with the charge of a full-grown wolf. Idun called Skoll off before he killed the man, and he was allowed to escape to spread the word of the great wolf that protected the Onodaga.

Twelve years had passed since the Onodagas entered this valley. There had been peace for the most part but as all the small tribes became stronger, raids on each other were more frequent. A life for a life became the way of the savage, a code of honor that they came to live by. All these southern tribes became Iroquois. They were descended from the Huron but never again would they be Huron. The hatred ran so deep it would spill over into war for many centuries.

Thorfinn, Wildflower and their two daughters longed for word of Thor. Misty wanted to see her big brother again, he of the blue eyes like hers. In the fall of the year when the forest was ablaze with color and the cool winds of winter could just be felt in the early mornings, a large canoe loaded with furs carrying three men was seen approaching from the north. An outlying scout spied them from the woods and he hurried to the village with his news. One of the men had yellow hair like Thorfinn.

Thorfinn and his family raced through the woods to the lake's shore. This could mean but one thing, news of Thor or beyond all joy Thor himself. When the men in the canoe spotted them they turned their craft in towards shore and soon beached their canoe. Thor jumped out and grabbed his father with such gusto they both fell into the water laughing and shouting. It was then his mother's turn, but this greeting was more tender. Wildflower led him to Misty Dawn and he fell to his knees in front of her. How wonderful to have a beautiful sister such as she. Misty grabbed her brother and hugged him tight, his blue eyes flashed in the sunlight; he was her brother, no doubt of that.

Chapter 17

"Where in this land did you find skins and hides such as these?" Thorfinn asked his son. "These are huge like a bear only much heavier and warmer than even the bear."

Thor said, "These animals, the Indians call them buffalo, are roaming all over the plains and valleys that we have journeyed to. I bring the best for my family and the rest for trading. I am glad I found you again; I thank the great Master of life."

"I see Gray Owl and Bard are here with you; I hope the others are well," exclaimed Wild Flower.

"They were all well when we last saw them--that was quite a time ago. We have been a far distance but I had to see my family again."

Bard stood by the canoe and whenever he thought no one noticed he stole a glance at Misty. How beautiful she was, he thought.

They all unloaded the canoe carrying the hides to the village. Each elder was presented with one to his delight. Lame Duck received one also, a warm comfort for an old man during the cold season.

Thorfinn gathered all the people together. This night would be a celebration on the safe return of Thor and his companions. "Light all the fires," he shouted, "and let venison be put on all the cooking spits.

Tonight we hear the strange tales of these brave men. Let all who would hear these wondrous stores listen well. These will be tales to tell your grandchildren."

Grey Owl let out a whoop; he would bring much honor to his clan when the story was told. Several warriors began the low steady beat of the drums. These drums called the people together. People gathering corn from the fields afar heard the beat to return to camp. No one wanted to miss out on this great event.

Thor, Bard, and Grey Owl were seated at the place of honor reserved for those who earned great respect by their deeds.

Misty Dawn seated herself across from her brother and Bard, the low flames of the fire flickering between them. When all were quiet Thorfinn rose and spoke, "Let us hear of the deeds of Thor--he of the blue eyes, Bard and the brave Grey Owl. Let them be honored as befits them." He seated himself again and with a gesture towards Thor bid him rise and speak.

"I am Thor son of Thorfinn the Northman, son of Wildflower and brother to the Onadaga. He began. "Many seasons have passed since my brother, Grey Owl, and our Viking brothers left the northern woods sailing away on the great lake Ontario in our brother's ship

We sailed west following the coast. Many times we went ashore to explore the forests, which are beautiful like our own spruce forests

Finding no sign of other men we constantly sailed west. After several week's journey, sometimes thorough very strong rough seas, we entered a large river. We floated with the current and lite sail as the water ran swift here. As the current became stronger we put the ship to shore tying her to a large tree. We went on foot for several miles fearing rapids because of the fast-flowing water." Here he paused, darting his eyes around the listeners. Everyone was eager for him to continue.

Thor smiled and resumed his speech. "As the ship was secured we walked the river's bank. The fast-flowing water became stronger and stronger. The mist began rising high in the sky and a roar so loud we could not speak without yelling. We then came to a small rise in the land. On reaching the top we beheld a sight that will live in our minds forever. The river roared and rushed over gigantic water falls. Rainbows floated in the mist, the roar of falling water was deafening. If we had not secured the ship when we did all would have been loss, the ship nor none of us could not have survived these mighty falls." Thor paused and then said, "I will let Gray Owl speak now for all should have a part in the telling of this adventure."

Thor seated himself next to Bard who seemed to be unaware of anything except Misty Dawn.

Grey Owl rose and raising his arms to the sky began. "Thank the Great Spirit for delivering us from that mighty river. Its wonders are too great to describe or believe.

"We returned to the ship, we could neither go forward nor retrace our way back to the lake for the current was too strong. We had to leave the ship to travel on foot; we carried all that we could food, tools, weapons. We were determined not to be turned back by these great falls. We journeyed around the falls gazing in wonder at their majesty as we went. Following the river at the base of the falls for several days we came upon a large birch tree forest. Here we built five strong canoes for our journey. We built these canoes while our Viking brothers stripped the bark from the trees. We then paddled west across another large lake and upon reaching the other side entered the thick forests growing there. This land was flat unlike our hills and mountains, but fertile and rich still. We saw much game of all kinds--food was no problem for us. We headed west still following the sun. Thor had heard rumors of a mighty river said to lie this way. We agreed to find it before we turned back towards our homelands."

Bard remained seated, as he could not speak the Iroquois tongue very well. Some words he had mastered but he would not embarrass himself in front or the whole village, especially Misty, by stuttering and stammering with his words. He was still a young lad, just a couple of years older than Misty.

Gray Owl continued. "We came upon some people, they called themselves Illini. Their speech being alike to the Huron we soon learned to converse with them. They were a friendly people and welcomed us as brothers. This then is where we have been, living with these people, exploring their lands and gathering these mighty hides we brought back with us. Our Viking brothers are with them still for their maidens were beautiful to behold. They have all taken wives and are content to stay there. Only Bard has not taken a bride, being so young. I also have turned my heart towards my home and people and one who is here."

With that his glance fell on a young girl, seated with her mother, watching Grey Owl intently; returning his glances with a smile.

He continued his story by telling of their return, going to the place where they had secured the ship, which was no longer there, its fate still unknown

They felt that some roving band of Indians had come across it tied to the trees, possibly cutting her free in fear of the ferocious dragon head on the bow, its fate surely met by going over the great falls, never to be seen again.

At the conclusion of Grey Owl's speech all the elders stepped forward grunting their approval. No one of their tribe had ever ventured so far before; no one even dreamed of people farther west on the plains or a wonder such as the falls.

It was late when everyone sought his or her sleeping mats. All had their bellies full of deer meat and many other good things. Many bowls of strong brew, which they made from corn, had been consumed. Now it was time for sleep. Sentries were posted for a sharp watch still had to be kept. Smoke from dying fires drifted skyward. All was quiet and still, at least for the present, the embers glowing bright orange slowly succumbed to a gray ash by morning.

Chapter 18

The next morning Thor walked with his father on the shore of the lake, mist still rose from the calm, still surface as the calls of the loons echoed through the woods. The sun was just peeking over the horizon causing the forest to stir with life. Thorfinn always enjoyed the early mornings when the birds broke out with their songs. This was the time when peace seemed a reality and one could fully appreciate God's hand in creating such a masterpiece.

"Father do you still try to teach the people about Christ and the new religion?"

"I have not spoke long or hard on this, Thor. The people seem to desire a messiah of their own race to come and lead them to peace. They believe the great spirit, creator of all, can do this for them if he so desires and I believe they might be right. Jesus came for all men but it's hard for them to understand. The Mohawks are constantly warring on us and our young men strike back whenever they can despite my efforts to curb the warfare." Thorfinn continued talking to his son as they walked along the shore. What a fine young man Thor had grown to, a kind heart full of compassion but combined with the strength of a Viking, a man who thought of others and their welfare before himself.

"When I return to the plains I plan to teach the people there about Christianity. They have their beliefs which I respect greatly but the two different forms of religion are really the same--the belief in one God that created all and a sincere reverence for nature."

"Do you mean to leave us so soon, my son?" Thorfinn asked with a look of disappointment.

"I must," said Thor. "The woman I mean to make my wife waits for me even now. If not for the danger of the trip back here I would have brought her with me but I knew not what we would find or what dangers might arise." He paused and then continued. "I do not believe my friends will be returning with me, however. Grey Owl has his heart set on someone here and I believe young Bard will be paying you a visit soon. His thoughts are on Misty day and night. He is a brave young man, father, a man to be trusted in all things." Thorfinn listened for he knew this day would come. "You lose a son again but perhaps gain a brave man for husband for Misty." Thor grinned as he said this and Thorfinn smiled also.

Sure enough that evening Bard visited Thorfinn and his family as they sat by their fire in front of their lodge. Misty kept her eyes glued to the burning embers knowing what Bard meant to ask her father. If Thorfinn did not grant permission for them to marry her world would be shattered, or so she thought.

Bard greeted everyone inquiring as to their health and then gaining the courage he needed he spoke straight to Thorfinn. "Thorfinn, I wish to ask your blessing for Misty and myself to be married, we both desire it very much. I will protect her with my life, care for her every need and do my best to make her happy all the days of our lives." Looking at both Thorfinn and Wildflower he continued, "I wish to stay here in the forest the rest of my life. No longer do I desire to return to Greenland for I feel more at home here in the woods and mountains than anywhere else. If you grant me this great honor of marrying your daughter I will forever be in your debt." Having said this he took a seat close to Misty and they both looked anxiously at Thorfinn waiting in anticipation for his reply.

The Northman looked at Bard straight in the eyes as one honorable man would to another and replied, "Bard, I know you to be an honest man and your heart is true. If this is what my daughter desires I grant my permission gladly. We welcome you to our family with open arms and glad hearts. May your life together be long, happy and blessed with many children."

Bard grabbed Misty giving her a big hug. He also hugged Wildflower and then grasped Thorfinns arms and thanked him over and over until Thorfinn laughed. He knew his daughter was getting a brave Viking warrior that would protect her and make her happy.

The next day preparations were begun for the wedding. Thor would delay his departure until after the marriage ceremony for he wanted to share in the fun of building a lodge for his sister and her new husband to be. The whole village pitched in; everyone wanted to help. With all these well-meaning hands the new lodge was constructed in only two days time, a fresh new lodge smelling of fresh spruce, warm and cozy. Bard, Thor and Grey Owl had also constructed a small hut south of the village close to the shore of the lake where the two young lovers would greet each other as man and wife with only the forest looking on.

A hunt was organized for meat to feed all the village for this was to be a celebration like no other. Thor would be leaving after the wedding so it would be a special time for two reasons. When all was ready the ceremony was held on a beautiful spring morning near the lakes shore. Lame Duck and another elder asked the Great Sprit's blessing on their union as he passed his eagles wing over their heads. With that they were joined together for all time to be as one on this earth forever. When the ceremony was concluded everyone returned to the village for the great feast that had been prepared for all. It would be late in the day before Bard and Misty could steal away in his canoe to the special place he had prepared for them. All was well for now as life should be.

The next day Thor began his preparations for his journey back to the plains. Two young warriors eager to make the journey with him helped pack his canoe with provisions for the long trip. The two young men spoke to Thor expressing their desire to journey with him; the stories that were told around the campfire had caught their imagination, fueling a desire to see these far off places and people.

"We would be honored if he of the blue eyes would take us with him. We will not desert you and perhaps we will be of great help to you."

Thor replied, "I will be happy to have my brothers with me. It is a long journey and you might never see these woods again. Think well on this and if you still wish to come with me you shall be welcome." Thor told his father and mother goodbye once again. He showed his father the crude compass he had taken from the ship. With this he could cut across country saving many miles. He promised to return again someday perhaps to stay with his new wife.

Lame Duck Dancing for Good Luck on the Hunt

Thorfinn and Lame Duck warned him to be careful for he would be traveling through Senacas and Mohawks and both tribes were warring on everyone that crossed their lands. The next morning Thor and his two companions dipped their paddles in the calm lake waters while waving goodbye to everyone. As they disappeared from sight the village returned to its daily routines as much had to be done like always.

Chapter 19

All the people were warned to be alert, to take care while working in the fields, hunting or whatever chore carried them too far from the village. Armed warriors kept a constant watch on the woods surrounding the village and the cleared fields. Having built the village on a hill gave them a big advantage on watching all ways for an enemy's approach. Small bands of warriors also scouted through the woods towards the land of the Mohawks searching for any sign of roving war parties.

The high, palisaded walls of the village combined with only one narrow entrance offered some security to the people; at least they would stand a chance to defend themselves in the event of an attack. The Mohawks were very strong, many warriors could be assembled for war if they so desired. Most of the people felt they had not suffered an attack thus far due to the legend of Thorfinn, the yellow haired demon from the north; his strange mighty weapons and wondrous deeds had been told and retold around many campfires. This also increased the Mohawks desire to kill him--great would be the glory for the man or men who struck him down. Warriors talked and dreamed of this constantly, working their courage up to attempt it. One such brave was "the Otter" known for his cunning and swiftness among the Mohawks. He above all desired to confront Thorfinn and claim the glory for his kill. His claim to be a war chief could not be denied if he killed the yellow haired Northman. He had been talking to many braves for many months planning an attack on the Onadaga village. The plan was to approach thru the swamps south of the village and gain the element of surprise by a sudden rush from the woods, a quick surprise to over run the town before a strong resistance could be mounted against them. Victory would surely be theirs; the woods would ring with their victorious war cries. The plan seemed good to many and a war dance was held around a huge fire in the center of their village. Each man came forth to strike the war post with his hatchet and recount his previous deeds on the warpath. The huge force was assembled and made ready. A hundred mile trek lay before them but they traveled light carrying only their weapons, for they would live off the land until the battle which would yield all the food they would desire when they were victorious. In the full bloom of summer the giant forest swallowed them up and hid them so no man could tell they were even there gliding quietly through the trees as like a giant shadow spreading across the ground. Avoiding Onodaga scouts was absolutely necessary if the attack was to work as planned.

Early one morning as the village awoke and people going about their daily chores, a young warrior scouting the swamps south of the village was lucky enough to see the advance party of the Mohawk band. He saw three fiercely painted warriors slipping through the trees, but they failed to notice him. The young Onodaga slipped down into the brush and made his way hurriedly back to the village. As he crossed the open fields he raised the alarm to everyone he could. He was only a young boy but this day would see him honored as a full-grown warrior. On reaching the village he quickly sought out Thorfinn telling him what he had seen. He knew not how many more might be coming but Thorfinn was taking no chances. He raised his horn and blew loud and clear calling all to get ready for battle. Once the Mohawks heard the horn they knew their surprise had failed but feeling strong in numbers they determined to attack at once.

Ladders were quickly cut and lashed together to scale the walls. As they knelt at the forest edge the Otter's eyes gleamed with the lust for battle. One by one the Mohawk warriors began their fearsome cries hoping to strike fear in their enemies hearts. The woods seemed to be alive with shrikes and yells from every side--the village was surrounded. As the village prepared for the first attack the cries increased to blood-curdling screams, if not for the young scouts warning the village would have been over run for sure. Warriors mounted the walls preparing to fire their arrows at the onrushing Mohawks. Thorfinn grabbed his sword but in his haste he left the scabbard behind. When he realized this he had no time to return for it; he would have to fight without it.

The Mohawks attacked with a vengeance, throwing firebrands over the walls to set fires among the huts causing much confusion. Women and children threw water on the fires trying to keep them under control. The braves on the walls fired their arrows in quick succession killing many as they ran across the fields. The attackers were many but the Onodagas were just as determined and fierce. They would not yield their village as long as one man was alive among them. Mohawks reached the walls with their ladders; climbing to the top and dropping to the ground inside. Hand-to-hand combat broke out everywhere; tomahawks crushing skulls of attackers and defenders alike.

Thorfinn, Bard and Grey Owl fought side-by-side turning back one onslaught after another; if they stayed close to each other no one could penetrate the gate. The fighting grew thick and heavy, more and more warriors charged the three defenders, their faces painted with the lust for a kill; a strong heart was needed to stand and resist.

Thorfinn engaged one warrior rushing at him, his war club poised in the air for a killing blow. If he could kill the Northman he would be honored above all others. Thorfinn turned to meet his rush; planting his feet he caught the warriors blow on his sheild, at the same time plunging his sword into the heart of the savage. As he met this warrior he failed to see another about to throw his lance. Grey Owl turned in time bending his bow to its fullest, sending a shaft straight into the Mohawk as he ran towards Thorfinn causing him to fall dead at his feet. Thorfinn turned to see if Grey Owl was all right, his eyes afire with the lust for battle, his Viking blood running hot through his veins.

The Mohawks were starting to retreat back into the swamps knowing they were beaten. Several were killed as they ran, the archers letting their shafts fly true as fast as they could. Thorfinn raised his arm calling for enough. The village was safe for now; they had been blessed with victory. Even as the wounded were being cared for several braves clamored for a raid on the Mohawks. Young hot-headed braves did not want to listen to Thorfinn's talk of peace. Revenge was on their minds. He saw that his tales of Christ were not being listened to. It would take someone of their own race to unite them.

Chapter 20

This time the Onadaga had triumphed, the Mohawks had to retreat back into the swamps and forest from which they came. The tall palisades of the village and the combined strength of the two Vikings defending the gate had proved too much for the Mohawks. The Otter glared from the woods, his eyes gleamed with hatred for the Northman. He was looking for the glory to be received from killing Thorfinn, not disgrace for retreating unsuccessful from the battle. He would return soon with more warriors if necessary; victory must be his.

Many of the young Onadaga warriors wanted to pursue the Mohawks into the swamps but Thorfinn restrained them, they would lose many lives in such an action, better to stay strong to resist the next attack should it come which they knew would happen.

Thorfinn barely realized that he had left his scabbard on his mat. This time it had not made a difference, he survived the battle but he wondered if there was any truth in the old Viking legend or was it just a myth handed down through the generations; he determined not to let the myth of the scabbard prey on his mind ever again.

Bard had fought well along side Thorfinn, a fearsome pair indeed when aroused though they preferred peace among the tribes if possible. Grey

Owl was also praised for his quickness and courage. He had saved the life of Thorfinn and the Northman thanked him. The rest of the year was quiet; the Mohawks were recovering from their losses while life went on in the village. Grey Owl and his wife had a new baby boy whom they named Hiawatha. No one could guess what a future he had in store for him for some day he would be the spokesman for the great peace Thorfinn always talked of, an eloquent speaker and orator of the Iroquois people.

Thorfinn was getting on in years now but he felt the tribe was in good hands with Grey Owl and Bard. Lame Duck spent most of his time setting by the fire ready to tell the stories of his youth to anyone willing to listen, especially the stories of his adventures with Thorfinn.

Thorfinn thought hard for a way to stop the warring between his tribe and the Mohawks. To just sit and wait for another attack was foolish; there must be something he could do. Many hours were spent walking alone in the forest, setting by a fast moving stream or staring out across the lake. Then one day it came to him: the main force behind the Mohawks' aggression was the hatred of the Otter, their feared war chief. Thorfinn would journey to the land of the Mohawks and challenge him to single combat such as the Vikings did to settle disputes. If he was successful perhaps things would settle down for a while for it was rumored even some of the Mohawks were tired of constant warfare. The Otter was keeping them inflamed; he was the one that needed to be stopped.

Thorfinn told Bard of his plan, at first Bard feared for Thorfinn's life but the Northman convinced him it was the only way. He could not sit by and take a chance on all his loved ones being killed in another attack. Wildflower too tried to dissuade him but she also knew her husband once his mind was made up.

Two brave young Onodaga warriors volunteered to carry a wampum belt to the Mohawks' village calling for a council where Thorfinn could put forth his challenge. The two warriors made ready and left the next morning. If all went well they would return in six days time. Honor demanded that they not be harmed while offering a belt of peace. Thus it was that they departed following the lakeshore south towards the Mohawk river.

Thorfinn busied himself preparing for the fight to come. Hours were spent in the sweat lodge combined with long swims in the lake. He meant to be in his top fighting strength, sharp and alert. Grasilda would be his weapon for this battle--he always felt strong when this mighty Viking sword was in his hands. Wildflower had sewn two strong deer hides together to form a vest that would protect him from many knife wounds. The Otter was known for fighting with his knife in one hand and tomahawk in the other; he was equally good with each weapon and Thorfinn had his work cut out for him. Grey Owl practiced many hours rushing in with both weapons at close quarters helping Thorfinn react to the attacks and honing him to razor sharpness.

Two weeks passed before the two young warriors returned late one evening with the news that the Otter had accepted Thorfinn's challenge. They were to meet mid day between their two lands seven days from now. Thirty warriors from each tribe would be present but this was a matter of honor, the winner would walk away without trouble. Thorfinn took Grey Owl and thirty warriors with him; Bard was left behind to guard the village in case of treachery. The night before their departure was spent around the campfire as Thorfinn explained to the people that a real chance for peace might come out of this if he won the battle, and if he lost perhaps the Otter's hatred would be satisfied. If not then Bard and Grey Owl might have to lead the people farther east and start anew. Young Hiawatha sat at his father's side listening to all that was being said still unaware of the part he was to play in all these events someday.

The sun rose red in the heavens as the small band departed the village. The two warriors who had acted as messengers led the way for they knew the site where the fight would take place. They would follow the lake shore as far as possible to lessen the chance of ambush. The feeling was that the Mohawks could be trusted in this matter but many still had their doubts. On the sixth day just before dark they broke into a large clearing caused by wind and fire. This was the place where the two combatants were to meet the next day. Scouts brought back word that the Mohawks were encamped in the woods on the other side; all seemed to be as it should. The next morning Thorfinn was the first to step out into the clearing and walk towards the center. Drawing Grasida from her scabbard he banged on his shield twice shouting out, "I am Thorfinn the Northman, let the Otter come forward to meet me in battle if he dares."

The Otter stood in the shadows working up his hatred, he meant to kill the Northman today, his yellow hair would adorn his lodge tonight and great would be his glory. All would honor him for the mighty warrior he was, and then he would destroy the Onodagas once and for all. As Thorfinn issued his challenge the Otter let out his most ferocious war whoop and came charging across the clearing brandishing his tomahawk in one hand and knife in the other. He meant to bowl Thorfinn over with the rush of his charge and sink his tomahawk into his head. As he ran toward Thorfinn screaming his war cry Thorfinn planted his feet waiting for the Otter to close. The Mohawk swung his tomahawk with all his might. Thorfinn raised his shield taking the full blow as the Otter crashed into him slicing at his chest with his knife. They both fell backward but Thorfinn was the first on his feet in an instant turning to deliver the fatal blow from his sword. The Otter stared in disbelief at the sword as it plunged through his body, his eyes looking at Thorfinn with a hatred too deep to fathom. He gasped his last breath and fell dead at the Northman's feet. The Onodagas let out their victory yells causing the woods to reverberate with their screams. Thorfinn raised his hand calming them down. This had been a matter of honor; this would be the end of it. "Enough, no more, let this be the end of the fighting. A brave warrior lost his life here today. Let his fellows bear his body away in peace as we agreed." Thorfinn spoke to them all as he walked away from his fallen foe. Grey Owl greeted him by clasping his arm, no words had to be spoken. Each knew how the other felt. The Mohawks carried the Otter into the forest, disappearing into the woods as if they had never been there. If they lived up to their word peace would prevail for a time however short it might be.

Chapter 21

Life settled down to a peaceful existence, Bard and Misty were very much in love never leaving one another's side for long. The entire village helped Bard build his new hut for Misty. It was the finest looking hut in the village and Misty was very proud of it. Grey Owl also received a helping hand in the construction of his new hut for he planned to take a wife soon also.

At night most of the people sat around the main campfire in the center of the village, talking or just enjoying the fire and companionship. As the thousands of stars glittered in the night sky life seemed to be serene at last. The people felt more secure than they had in a long time. Sentries and scouts still kept watch and patrolled the woods with a sharp watch; the Mohawks could return any time and Thorfinn meant to be ready if they did. Young Hiawatha was growing tall and showed a distinct talent for speaking to people at councils; he was wise beyond his years. Peace eventually came to an end as tribes farther west began invading the forest in their area--Huron, Seneca, Abanaki among others, all warlike, constantly attacking each other. All Thorfinn and Bard could do was to protect their village from attack by staying vigilant. A rumor was adrift in the forest that told of one man from the north, a Huron child rejected by his own people. Something was different about him. It was said the Great

Spirit favored him and great things could be expected from him. Thorfinn wondered if this could be the man of his vision, the man to bring peace to all the forest people at last. He hoped and prayed it would be so.

Warfare changed somewhat to where individual warriors sought vengeance on each other for various transgressions taken against them or their clan; it was an eye for an eye, a life for a life, with no end or solution in sight. Thorfinn and his family managed a good life for themselves and their people, his reputation as a warrior helped deter many who would otherwise have tried to harm them. Hiawatha was approaching manhood and was soon to wed, the next few years would be grievous for him driving him out of the village to live as a hermit in the vast wilderness where his life long work for all people really began. Thorfinn had led a full life filled with adventure. He never forgot the people that saved his life, devoting his life to helping them survive. He had been the first Viking to mingle with the forest dwellers and explore the vast wilderness of the great lakes. His family brought him much joy as he watched them grow through the years for they were truly a close loving family. Hiawatha had married and his wife bore him several children whom he loved very much. One day as he and his little family were traveling through the forest to go hunting, an evil jealous man from his own village killed his wife and children while Hiawatha was stalking a deer through the woods. Hiawatha was so devastated by this he ran farther into the dismal wilderness of the Adirondacks never wanting to see people again. Thus it was that the great mystic from the north found him in his grief and changed his life forever. The evil man that destroyed his family was made an outcast from the village but he still stayed close by in the forest. His life, too, would be changed by the great peacemaker.

Chapter 22

During the following years the Hurons, Senacas, and Mohawks warred among themselves constantly, also with all other tribes in the area. Warfare raged among all people in the forest.

The Iroquois people, who were at one time part of the Huron family, all were driven out to what is now upper New York State, the vast wilderness of the Adirondacks.

The first people created by the Master of life had fallen to the uttermost depths of life, both physical and moral; but there were those that remembered the legend of a messiah to come and save them from their despair.

At last just such a messiah did appear to them out of the northern wilderness. He brought a teaching that stirred their hearts with hope. He had a plan for fulfilling the Master of life's will and instilling it into their human relations.

The messiah's name was "Degandawida," he the thinker. He was to lay the groundwork for the great peace, which white men later called the league of five nations.

He was a prophet, saint, mystic and poet from the spruce forested land of the Iroquois.

The legend of Degandawida has him being born the son of a virgin mother whose family had become extinct. He had no clan or nation, only his mother. Her name in English meant, "she has a new face, pure and spotless."

She was born with an omen believed by many to foretell of a special destiny, and she knew only the companionship of her old widowed mother. As she approached womanhood a child stirred in her womb yet she had never been with a man.

Her mother did not believe her story, berating her and beating her until the poor girl spent her days and nights weeping.

One night a luminous figure appeared to her in a dream. The child about to be born would one day unite his people in peace. Her mother saw only evil before them so she tried to destroy the newborn child by cutting a hole in the ice and submersing him in the ice-cold river. The child would not sink and suffered no ill effects from this. Everything she tried was supernaturally thwarted.

The boy grew up lonely, neglected and persecuted in the wilderness with only his mother to teach him. She believed in his divine mission and taught him love and gentleness. She infused in him a sense of high destiny. He grew to be a very handsome man whose face reflected one of the world's great souls. He had one major flaw, however; he stammered and stuttered badly.

This did not deter him as he had his vision. He saw a gigantic spruce tree which represented the sisterhood of humanity. Its roots were to be the five tribes of the Iroquois. An eagle perched on top of it, watching constantly for any enemy who came to disturb the peace.

His own people would not accept him for he had no clan, so he left his mother's bark hut north of Ontario and traveled to the land of the Mohawks, "the flint people." The Mohawks had always been the most aggressive as well as the most progressive of all the forest nations.

All the tribes were warring with each other as their code of honor provided no means of ending the strife. Tribal traditions demanded a life for a life and animosity had reached such a point that no settlement could ever be made to end it.

The Mohawk elders were in despair. As if in answers to their prayers the tribeless messiah Degandawida appeared out of the wilderness.

At first his vision of uniting all the tribes in peace was received with much skepticism and misgivings, but this did not discourage him.

To prove he was the prophet he claimed to be, he climbed to the top of a tall pine on the edge of a deep gorge. The Mohawks then chopped the tree down. He fell with the tree into the gorge but within minutes climbed out back to the top unhurt.

Everyone present then believed him. He was the messiah they had longed for. The Mohawks accepted him, listened to his teachings, and readily turned to his ideas. Their close neighbors with whom they warred constantly were the Onodagas.

They wanted to believe his vision and this was the time he met the man who would be his voice and disciple, Hiawatha.

Hiawatha was a grief-crazed wanderer, an Onodaga warrior whose wife was killed by a fiendish man, feared by the whole tribe. He had even killed seven children. He received little sympathy from his fellow tribesmen for they had many problems of their own.

He went to live as a hermit in the woods and it was at this point he was found by Degandawida.

The messiah brought genuine comfort and understanding to Hiawatha who underwent a complete conversion, his sorrow and hate swept away by the great man's words.

He taught Hiawatha to love his enemies and do good to those who would use him spitefully. Hiawatha then went to the evil man who had killed his family. This man was known as Ododarkoh. From Hiawatha's words he changed the man completely, converting him to their cause. He, too, became a devoted disciple of Degandawida and was named the firekeeper of the Onodagas, a position of high honor and respect.

Degandawida's vision was that of a titanic spruce tree whose upper branches broke through the sky into the everlasting light of the elder brothers. The tree grew out of a luminous snow-white carpet spread over rock-strewn hills. The roots of the tree were the five tribes. An eagle perched on top to watch for trouble from any direction.

All men of all races could find sanctuary upon it. The soil that the tree grew on was composed of three double principles: NE Skenno, health of body and sanity of mind, peace between individuals and groups; NE Gaiihwiyo, righteousness in conduct, thought, and deed, equity and justice in human rights; NE Gashedenza, maintenance of self-defense and military power, maintenance of spiritual power.

War as they knew it had been the quarreling of children. These forest mystics had no concept of more bitter quarreling over land, power, and gold. This led to the eventual downfall and failure of their dream.

When the agreement among all the tribes was finalized, Degandawida put his seal of approval on it. His words were as follows, "So now we have put this evil from the earth. Verily, we have cast it deep down into the earth. I am indeed Degandawida and with the confederate lords of the five nations I plant the tree of Great Peace. I plant it in your territory, Ododarhoh, and in that of the Onondaga nation, in the territory of which you are the firekeeper.

"I name the tree the Tree of the Great Long Leaves, and under the shade of this tree of the Great Peace we spread the soft, white, feathery down of the globe thistle as seats for you and your cousin lords, Ododarhoh. Here shall you sit and watch over the council fire.

"Roots have spread out from the great tree of peace. If any man of any nation outside of the five nations shall desire peace, to obey the laws of the Great Peace he may trace the roots to their source and he shall be welcome to take shelter under the Tree of the Long Leaves.

"The shadow of the tree will be pleasant and beautiful. Never again shall man walk in fear. All the peoples of mankind will dwell there in peace and tranquility, for all will deposit their minds there. We will have one tongue, and one blood in our bodies. And at the top of the tree sits Skajirna, the eagle. He watches all ways and will warn us when he sees approaching that which brings destruction and death.

"A council fire for this law shall be kindled for all nations. It shall be kindled for the Cherokees and for the Wyandottes. We will kindle it also for the seven tribes living towards the sun rising and these nations shall light such fires for the peoples living still further towards the sun rising. We will kindle the fire also for the nations that dwell towards the sun setting. All shall receive the Great Law and labor together for the welfare of man.

"So I, Degandawida, and the confederate lords now uproot the tallest pine tree and into the hole we cast all weapons of war. Into the depths of the earth and into the waters under the earth we cast all weapons of strife. We bury them from sight forever and plant again the tree. Now I shall be seen no more of men and I go whither none can follow me."

Having said these words to a large number of his devoted followers, he walked to the shore of Onondaga Lake where a canoe of stone, luminously white was drawn up on the beach. He paddled westward and his grieving followers watched from shore as the mystic craft disappeared in the sunset. Five years had passed since his coming; his thoughts had been of all mankind, not Iroquois-speaking people alone. Then Hiawatha sent missionaries east, west, north and south to all tribes. They returned with strings of colored shell, the original of wampum, Indian money invented by Hiawatha as a pledge of their acceptance of the Great Peace. Hiawatha lived to a ripe old age, spending his later years with the Mohawks. As he grew very old one day he entered a pure white birch bark canoe and paddled west across Lake Champlain to disappear into the giant spruce forests of the Adirondacks never to be seen again. The peace these two men brought to the forest people lasted over three hundred years. Only the coming of the white man with his greed, disease and lust for power destroyed it.

Thorfinn became an honorary elder of the Onodagas; his presence was required at all the great councils of the Iroquois League. Thorfinn lived to a ripe old age helping Hiawatha develop the league.

The vision was a beautiful concept for men to live together in peace, so much so that the founding fathers of our great country incorporated its principles in the Constitution of the United States of America. The eagle was also adopted as a symbol of vigilance and freedom. Perhaps if they are needed these forest mystics will return again to help guide men in their search for peace among all men.

The End

The Otter Charges Across the Clearing Towards Thorfinn

Historical references for this novel were gathered from *The Sagas of Icelanders and Wilderness Messiah* by Thomas R. Henry

"Dedicated to my loving wife Charlotte and to my children, grandchildren and great grandchildren"

www.ingramcontent.com/pod-product-compliance
Lightning Source LLC
Chambersburg PA
CBHW020615310726
48979CB00008B/1491/J

* 9 7 8 1 4 2 6 9 3 3 3 8 7 *